Verily

Rĕtta

TATE PUBLISHING
AND ENTERPRISES, LLC

Verily

Published by Tate Publishing & Enterprises, LLC
127 E. Trade Center Terrace | Mustang, Oklahoma 73064 USA
1.888.361.9473 | www.tatepublishing.com

Tate Publishing is committed to excellence in the publishing industry. The company reflects the philosophy established by the founders, based on Psalm 68:11,
"The Lord gave the word and great was the company of those who published it."

Cover design by Junriel Boquecosa
Interior design by Jake Muelle

Published in the United States of America

ISBN: 978-1-63367-451-6
1. Fiction / General
2. Fiction / Christian / General
14.11.04

To my best friend Holy Spirit

To my beloved husband

To my son Joseph, whose unselfish service to his family never fails to amaze me; my daughter April, who is the sunshine of my days; my daughter Priscilla, the most gentle of ladies and my continuing inspiration; my son Travis, who makes me laugh

To all my grandchildren today and to come

To my precious mother

To Pat, my mother-in-law, who is more like my sister

To my dad, who inspired the
Hank Benson of this story

To my sister and brother who are such a part of me

To all God's children…

Introduction

Raised in the Antelope Valley of Southern California, a high valley of the Mojave Desert, I, Rĕtta, remember the best childhood.

My dad bought me my first horse when I was ten years old—a one-eyed buckskin we named "Hualapai" (pronounced Wal-lah-pie) because of the Hualapai Indian reservation Dad was working on at the time in Arizona. The horse was old, and therefore the safest teacher for a young girl. It took much coaxing to urge him into a gallop, and only then, after a teeth jarring trot.

I would climb out of bed on days off from school, dress in my Western clothes, pull on my boots, and saddle that tall, worn-out cow horse by standing on our picnic table, enabling me to lift the thick blanket and heavy saddle upon his bony back. After securing the cinch strap around his middle and climbing on, we would be off into the desert morning, watching the sunrise as we headed out to the flat Joshua Tree covered valley or into the foothills.

If we chose the steep climb up Quartz Hill Mountain where the city water tank overlooked our town, my faithful friend made it without complaint. There I would step down from the stirrup and remove Hualapai's bit leaving the headstall looped around his neck to let him munch the tall, spring grass that grew in the shade of the Desert Juniper bush-like trees. Sitting beneath our favorite with its long strips of bark and small hard berries, the scent of munched grass from his worn teeth soon filled the cool air. It was then I stored memories of those lazy kid days that taught me to love my desert.

My desert. How I learned to know its every mood. The cold spring winds that caused the bright orange poppies to close their satiny peddles against it; the days when the summer sun burnt my skin while baking clean the grainy sand, too hot to walk barefoot upon; the welcome feel and smell of cool air pumping from the rotating fins of the swamp cooler.

So many days of summer I would clomp into my clean home, pigtails bouncing, and plop down upon the couch when my older sister would comment on my "horsey" smell and dusty boots, and Mama would only smile. After those lazy months ended, the shade trees would drop their brown and yellow leaves, rustling beneath our feet as we children dressed in Mom-made costumes carried our brown paper grocery bags from house to house for tricks-or-treats. Then, winter in the valley *might* bring a snow that was a reason for celebration because, *No School!* Snowmen, snow ball fights, wet socks for gloves on beet red hands, and towels laid out by the front door to wipe our muddy boots on. Then once again, the orange poppies would color the brown of the land, such a contrast against a sky so unbelievably blue, unless the sunset should set it on fire, a fire of color.

Memories. Could life be any greater? Trips with my family to the Sierra Mountain range where Daddy taught me to love every bit of God's mountains and Mama taught me to cook brook trout over a campfire. Then there were trips south from home to Grandma's and Grandpa's, my birthplace in Culver City, California, where the smell of the damp air will always send me back in time to a place so loved; a place of aunts, uncles, cousins, friends, and old dogs. Trips to the beach to learn a new feel of sun and breeze, different from my desert…beach sand in my clothes, white suds of natural ocean waves splashing against my young skin, teaching me to know yet another part of God's creation. All that I learned to feel growing-up has contributed to my enjoyment of story telling.

Las Vegas, Nevada? Sin City some may call it. I've known it as a child, and I've known it as an adult and have chosen to focus on the good in the town, meeting the kindest people there. And talk about being cared for by its workforce! It is truly a vacation place for a tired mother, as it has cared for me with clean beds, fine foods, beautifully groomed landscapes, and the chance to meet vacationers from every nation. It is like its own little world, and yes, there's bad there. But there is also good. So this is where the story of *Lea* begins. She finds the good in her world and its people, but Lea is no "pushover." Very much aware of the evil in the world, this lady will not let it keep her from her life's work.

Yes. Lea has learned as a young woman, what it took years for me, Rĕtta, to learn. It is a peace that I longed for when young, and prayed for, and now give thanks to Heavenly Father for this gift. I now live with the counsel of our Holy Spirit's wisdom and place my husband, children, grandchildren, mom and dad, sister and brother, you my family, and all his creatures great and small into his care. Then I sleep the content sleep of a child, knowing we have a Heavenly Father and Savior, Jesus Christ, who loves us and has sent Holy Spirit down from heaven to walk with us all the days of our lives. How wonderful is that?

Sincerely,
Rĕtta

1

"Hank! How can you expect me to trust my whole production to a kid? Do you have any idea how much money is tied up here? How many months I've worked to make it a success? The music industry is not kind to twenty-six-year olds running a show. Not only that, but there are important people here. These dance teams have traveled from all over the world. They could have brought in an orchestra from anywhere, but they chose mine!"

"You wanted my help, Jay. You asked for a miracle. Now you stand here in a sweat, arguing with me while that miracle is touching down at the airport in her own private jet this very"—Hank glanced at his watch—"this very minute. Okay. Now just listen. She's twenty-six years old but she is not a kid. She is a woman who learned to fly a plane from atop her daddy's lap while being weaned from her mama's milk. And she has the intelligence of—well—just trust me."

Jayson Rawlings, the production manager of *Summer's Night*, the new Las Vegas opening show and talk of the town, threw up his hands. "So you told her she's hired?"

"I told her I needed help for a friend whose Vegas production was on the line. She would do almost anything for me. I have no idea what it took for her to set her time aside, but she's here. So relax. She is the miracle worker you asked for."

Jayson clamped his lips together and glared at his old friend, a gesture Hank knew so well. There were a few moments where only the sound of band instruments were heard twanging onstage, tuning up for the early hours of rehearsal. Dancers' voices were heard in soft murmurs as they stretched and twirled in preparation for a grueling day of practice; but they needed music, and the lack of trust in their musicians' support was becoming evident. Even the stage crew was uncertain as to their duties in set preparation, knowing their temperamental manager was a perfectionist and was not pleased with the previous week's rehearsals—something just wasn't clicking.

Yes, the entire show made up of dancers from all over the world was dependent upon the small but important orchestra that should have been coordinating with them, but were being put off by a lack of unity. The entire team was a group of professionals that were not a team, and the disappointment in the spark that should have been there after three month's work made everyone restless. With only ten days until opening night, the establishment was looking to Jayson for an answer, and he knew well that Las Vegas, Nevada, the entertainment city of the world, was unforgiving when disappointed.

"Mr. Rawlings. You and Mr. Benson have a table setting here as requested."

Sarah Allan, Jayson's secretary and lady of quiet efficiency, expertly directed the two men to where a breakfast setting was neatly arranged upon a table positioned to the side of the stage. Here, her boss could oversee the morning's preparations. She knew better than to try and pry him from the showroom that would be his focus until the results were perfected, as was his way.

Sarah smiled to herself as he dug into the meal of scrambled eggs, hash brown potatoes, and fruit salad, sipping the rich black coffee between bites, the coffee he drank too much of. It was one of the many things in which she had no control over in his life.

Sarah oftentimes felt unappreciated instead of being recognized as a valuable asset by the man she had secretly loved the six years she had been in his employ. She rarely had time to watch him unobserved, and now her enjoyment was once again rudely interrupted by her workday.

"Ms. Allan, Mr. Dodson is on line three."

"Ms. Allan. You have a call—"

"Ms. Sarah. There is a gentleman in your office with a problem he says cannot await your attention—"

"*Stop*!"

Hank stood, his great height bringing attention to his presence along with the deep power of his voice. "*You three*! Put everyone on hold. Ms. Allan is out to breakfast for thirty minutes."

Reaching out, Hank took Sarah by the hand, directing her to his own seat and ordered her to "*eat*" from the plate he had just made for himself.

Jayson looked at the plate piled high with food and grinned at his speechless secretary. "Ms. Allan, I would advise you to do as you have been told or this Texan won't give you back to me until you do."

Hank settled at the end of the table. He watched Sarah's cheeks redden with the attention shown her. She wasn't an attractive woman as the world would label "attractive," but he thought her beautiful in her grace, cleanliness, work ethics, shyness, and love for a man who saw her only as a working machine.

She was tall for a woman, slight of build, while her greatest visual features were her large gray eyes and shy smile. He thought her blondish hair was also attractive in the neat professional way she twisted it back into an attractive kind of knot. But she had a sense of loneliness about her. He believed she had no family, and her shyness away from work kept her from having friends.

"So Sarah? What are your thoughts on the progress of *Summer's Night*?" Hank asked around a mouthful of potatoes.

Sarah glanced at Jayson who was focused hungrily on his meal, probably anxious to hurry back to his work.

"I can't seem to put my finger on it, Mr. Benson."

He made a comical face, making her smile. "I would ask you to call me Hank, but I'd be wasting my breath. Is that right, Jay?"

The focused Jayson was such a multitasker it made it possible for him to know pretty much of what went on around him at all times, thus making him the ideal production manager. He grinned. "She's irreplaceable, so stop flirting with her, old man."

"I'm not too old to flirt with a pretty woman any day of the week or time of the day," Hank said. Taking another huge bite of eggs and ham from a second plate of food he had made for himself, he glanced at his watch, feeling a quick rush of pleasure. The kid would be coming through the doors soon. It had been months since he'd seen her, though he kept track of her through her own secretary, Jerry Handly.

Jerry was a man who was Lea's overseer in all of her business affairs, a magic man with organizational skills that would make any want-to-be secretary weep. Needing very little sleep and with unbelievable computer knowledge, Lea depended on him so much, she confided once to him that Jerry was worth an office full of people, and Hank guessed that in her sense of fairness, she paid him thusly. But most importantly, he was a man of God. Loving the Lord Jesus first in his life as she did, united them continually; therefore, they were never at odds as how to handle her business affairs.

"So what is this kid like? Where did you meet her?" Jayson asked, watching the older man with interest. He liked and respected him. For all his toughness, Hank loved people. He had a gentleness that went beneath the gruff, old school exterior; and like a crazy old mine shaft, if one looked deep enough, he would find treasures in the man's life experiences.

He did have sadness in his years that could have broken him down, but instead he clung to his belief in the goodness of people. And the most extraordinary find about the complicated man was that Hank did not believe in death. To quote him in his word of faith would be that Jesus Christ gave us the gift of life. "Don't fear the death of this body, son," he once said. "When we lose our earthly body is when we break free to true freedom. Believe in Christ Jesus, and you will never die."

Jayson needed to hear those words when he was a young soldier going into battle. Hank taught him about his faith at a time when he needed the strength to overcome a terrible fear of dying. And since he became a Christian, and no one would argue a struggling one; nevertheless, he had overcome that terrible blood-sweating fear ever since.

Now his old friend gulped a mouthful of coffee, sucked at his teeth for a moment in thoughtfulness, and gazed off somewhere into his past. Jayson hid a grin. Hank Benson looked ever so much like an 1800s cowboy sheriff stepped off a black-and-white TV screen. From his abundant gray hair that always seemed to need a trim to his long sheriff mustache, he was a character figure to behold which always served him well with his fans in his very successful singing career.

Now Hank took a deep, thoughtful breath as he smoothed down his long mustache. "Who is Lea Ann Renton? Well boy, she is complicated, I can tell you that much. She showed up at the party of a musician friend in Missoula, Montana, and I got her to tell me her age, which was no easy feat. I had guessed it at twenty-five and was amazed when she confessed to me that she was eighteen years old. One look in those clear blue-green eyes told me she was a rare one of truth. There is a dignity within her that I could not fathom then and cannot fathom now only to say that I have never met a finer Christian woman. And that's how I thought of her, as a woman, when most girls her age would only be play acting at a late-night party.

"I could tell she trusted me from the start. Yea, she wasn't talkative even to me and less to the others there, but I knew she liked me. And it was instant friendship and has been ever since. Now when people first meet her, they get the impression that she's unfriendly, but she's just quiet.

"It would be helpful to keep in mind that Lea has an ability to learn, to remember detail. She's quick, sometimes blunt, but always fair and kind. She can learn anything she wants to but keeps quiet about her abilities. Music is her choice occupation. She can play just about any instrument and prefers working with small groups, especially youth groups. You would be amazed if you knew the number of songs she has written, and she sings many of her own. Her friends call her Lee. It is a masculine-sounding name she admits has opened more than a few doors for her because of the confusion. Now, you probably won't have much of a chance to get to know her, but it would be helpful if given the opportunity to speak with her at any length that she is a private person.

"Remember, Lea can be quiet but don't let her put you off. Also, she might dress tomboyish, but she's every inch a female. And I should tell you that my son

Karl will meet her for the first time tonight and will be sticking around to learn some about the music business. Yea, I know you and he aren't pals, but he'll stay in the background as usual."

Jayson smirked. "You'd think a retired marine medic shrink would have better things to do than hang out on a Las Vegas production line."

"Well—it's a long story. Here she is now."

Jayson glanced up to watch a most tailored dressed image of a top magazine model walk with natural long legged strides up the wide aisle of the showroom towards them. She had wispy, light blond hair that was cut very short and wore an almost completely male fashioned dark suit, black cop-like shoes, and carried a black leather briefcase in one hand. But as she approached their table, he found she had the most striking old-time Hollywood movie face of his dreams. When she smiled, her large blue-green eyes lit up most beautifully, and it was all for his craggy ole pal Hank. But instead of melting into his arms as most women did with the romancing guy in a gigantic bear hug, she held a slender hand out to him to be taken up in the most gentle handshake: like her hand was made of the finest porcelain.

"How are you, Hank?" She spoke easy, refined.

"Well, kid, now that I've seen the sun rise twice in one day, pretty great."

"Still the charmer."

"It's easy with you, lady."

The young woman shook her head, seeming unable to take her eyes off of him. After several long moments, she broke the spell.

"So, what's this terrible emergency?"

"It's standing here." He jerked his head sideways towards the gaping Jayson. "And this lovely lady gracing our breakfast table is Sarah, his secretary that I had to bully into relaxing for five minutes to dine with us."

"Have you eaten, Ms. Renton?" Sarah asked.

"Yes, Sarah. Thank you. My friends call me Lee."

When Lea focused her attention on Jayson, he was mesmerized by her eyes. They were so clear it seemed a man could tumble into them. But she was all business. With cool leadership always framed with respectfulness in tone and manner, she took the most plaguing problems of his day in control. Within nine hours, she had gained the trust of the entire team including his very capable secretary. And she seemed tireless, quietly composed, and quick to access and advise. By five o'clock, everyone was instructed in a no-nonsense manner to end their workday, focusing on food and rest while limiting any alcoholic beverages to three "moderate sized" drinks per off-time hours. Then with a "Sweet dreams. See you at seven sharp tomorrow morning!" she was gone as quickly as she had come.

Only then did Jayson realize that he had not discussed pay or contract with her and that his old friend Hank disappeared that morning after he had introduced him to the "Miracle" he had asked for.

2

Karl parked the rental car in the five-story garage. He had chosen the top floor farthest from the huge resort hotel/casino where his father was staying. Karl loved Hank and literally owed his life to him, but this favor was one that had him in a sweat. Of all the missions he had been on during his tour in the military overseas, he found himself feeling uncomfortable about fulfilling this simple favor to his dad.

After locking the doors of the rental car with a click of the small black device that the lady at the car rental desk had given him, he found the small button symbol used to pop open the trunk. The second key and clicker were tucked inside his snug Levis' pocket. Karl lifted two black suitcases from the trunk: one that held a dress suit and casual but neat-fitting clothing and one that held shoes for dress up, exercise clothing, and everything else he might need for the next three months. The one pair of black leather shoes would go with all of his clothing and the tennis shoes he now wore would also double for his workouts. He thought of how strangely light the tennis shoes felt after living so long in the tight lace-up military boots that had become such a part of his life.

Thinking of the favor he had to do for his dad as a "mission" to complete before settling into civilian life, Karl thought of his predicament and laughed aloud, surprising himself and a threesome of young women walking together to the parking garage elevator. The women had on their "glad rags," one of Hank's sayings. They glanced his way and somehow knowing it was party time in the city, began the flirtatious conduct some women acquire when dressed "fit to kill." *Dad! How many of your crazy old sayings have been engraved into my head. Now you've brought me to this place. Only you, Dad. Only you.* Karl had to laugh again. His love for the man was so great it was an ache deep in his chest. Looking around the place he thought about how Las Vegas was a vacation time for so many and work time for so many others that were glad to find it. But he, personally, was thinking of this night and coming months as a time to get over with.

This is for you, Dad. Then I'm off to the cabin to decompress.

It was getting dark, and Karl did not want to share the elevator with the three women who were showing enough cleavage to make him blush. As their perfume hung in the warm desert air like a vapor cloud, they held the metal elevator door opened for him to follow. But with a polite nod, he changed direction heading for the stairway. Stopping short of the entrance as the view of lights clicking on throughout the city caught his eye, he went to the railing to peer down over it. Las

Vegas was a city to behold at night. In the middle of the Nevada desert was bloomed *the* city of entertainment. Lights! They lit up the sky like a man-made sun. And water! Far below, fountains shot high into the air dancing with music he recognized as Mozart.

"Unbelievable," Karl whispered in awe. But as he breathed in the dry desert air, it brought to his mind the faces of the friends he had left behind in another desert landscape. Being a marine in the United States military gave him a sense of belonging, of purpose, for so long. And even with the tragedy of battle, he had known the finest of men, and his heart ached for having left them in the middle of a war. Perhaps he hadn't had time to properly mourn that separation. For the last few weeks, their faces, and even at times their voices, came to him at the strangest moments, seeming as if they were calling out to him.

But orders were orders. True, he must have been showing some kind of stress to have been sent home. True, he had tempted fate over and over in the field and still he lived. Was he being too reckless? Nevertheless, the ache was ongoing. He was not home by choice and knew enough about himself and his profession to see the signs of a deep and outrageous anger. His commanding officer was responsible for sending him home. And now on top of everything else, he was in the ultimate party town feeling like a "fish out of water." But now he had another job to do.

"Dad. It will be good to see you," Karl said to the quiet night settling in around the parking garage. It was time to begin his mission.

The casino was packed with people. Some were summer vacationers ready to spend money saved months in advance. Others were gamblers caught up into the game and dream of winning money, or for some, the disaster of losing it. They were men and women from their twenties to ninety years of age. Their dress was as varied as casual, to moderate, to richly adorned. But the strangest thing that caught Karl's keen eye was the range of nationality. The languages spoken were as diverse as a United Nations gathering.

The crowd seemed to be a cheerful one, including the drinkers of which there were plenty, especially because of the barelegged ladies in the eye-catching uniforms passing out alcoholic drinks everywhere. Card tables were set out in abundance, and the row upon row of talking slot machines that called out to him as he passed by made for an unbelievable racket

Keeping to the carpeted pathway made Karl think of the *Wizard of Oz* movie that he saw as a kid as he sat beside Hank in his large ranch home study. He had only been with Hank a short time. The child services agency that made it possible for him to be his father's son legally overlooked the fact that Hank was a single man. Maybe it was because of Hank's ability to give him a country-home life and educational opportunities. Though he didn't flaunt it, Hank had more income from his record and song writing career than most people, even his friends, knew about. People just liked him because he was one of the old characters that were becoming few and far between.

He was the first of Hank's adopted children and had been given several brothers since. "Needing to do some good with the gifts that the Lord has given me," Hank told him once, "make it possible for me to help boys have a good life growing up." And so he gave his adopted sons a ranch life, an education, and a sense of belonging. And that pleased Hank Benson as nothing else could.

Thinking of the good man who had taken him from a home for unwanted children to be a son to him, Karl smiled his rare smile at an elderly couple as he stepped aside to let them pass. He stood for a long moment watching them walk away hand in hand.

Hank was seldom thought of as "Father." He was "Dad" in every way. Although it had taken time for him as a kid to realize that Hank's love for him was genuine, when the truth finally sank in, he was "Dad" from that moment on.

"Excuse me!" Karl exclaimed as a young woman walked face first into his wide chest.

"Oh! I'm so sorry!" she stuttered.

Karl had reached out to steady the girl as she gazed up at him with adoring eyes. He thought her to be barely twenty-one, and as her girlfriends giggled, watching as he untangled her from his arms, his face warmed with discomfort. Having had such little contact with females since leaving on his overseas tour, he forgot how awkward these giggly youths could make him feel.

After another apology, he stepped past the group of girls and soon found himself out of the crowd and within the restaurant area that was less busy. Karl was looking for the casino coffee shop where he was to meet his dad. No fancy white-cloth restaurant for Hank Benson. And now for his meeting with the girl that his dad had tried for years to introduce him to. He suddenly felt like a kid again instead of a retired, cranky, marine doctor of thirty-four years of age. Well, he promised to spend a few months with her learning the music business, "Just to see if it might strike a note business wise," to quote his dad. Karl gritted his teeth wanting out of the situation as quickly as possible.

"Hey, son!"

"Dad," Karl greeted his father in a manly hug.

"You made good time. How was the flight?"

Karl shrugged. "Commercial."

Hank laughed. His marine son was not used to waiting in lines to catch a plane.

"We're seated back here out of the traffic. Busy place, and crowded, as big as it is."

"Yea. You need a GPS to get around," Karl said.

"You mean a compass?" Hank grinned.

Karl nodded. "The same."

"Thanks for humoring an old man."

"Don't give me that 'old man bit,' Dad."

"My bones aren't as kind to me as my kids are."

As they maneuvered around the people coming and going, waitresses balanced trays piled high with the dinner menu specials. The two tall men made their way to a corner table where Lea was finishing a call on her cell phone. Her eyes had not left them as they made their way across the room, but she knew immediately when Karl noticed her presence and felt his annoyance as keenly as if he had shouted it in frustration. For some reason it hit her as funny, which she was quick to hide as she ended her call to greet the much-talked-about son of her beloved old friend.

"Karl, meet the sweetest girl God forgot to glue wings on," Hank said as he sat beside her.

"Madam," Karl said with unsmiling coolness, so much a part of his nature.

"How do you do?" Lea reached over the table for a firm handshake before he sat down across from his father in the curved booth seat.

"Bet you're hungrier than a bitch wolf with twelve pups. We waited for you before ordering," Hank said.

After glancing at the menu, Karl placed it on the two stacked at the edge of the table, unconsciously neatening the stack with strong calloused fingers. The waitress came as if on cue taking Hank's order as he flirted his way through it; both Lea and Karl added their simple requests. The waitress picked up the menus but not before bestowing a pretty smile upon the solemn Karl.

Hank watched his dinner companions secretly throughout the meal, joking his way in an attempt to put them both at ease; although, they both behaved as he had expected. They were both themselves, quietly polite, while watchful and respectful as they were habitually with strangers. But Hank had set them both up beyond their expectations.

Both thought he planned secretly the same ending for their three months together, as he had indeed done in his heart for years. They were both such wonderful Christian people in their own individual ways. And Hank sent many prayers to Heavenly Father to bring the two together as helpmates. These two he had taken into his heart as his very special children. And there was always, of course, a danger in such a human love that he would lose his Lord's purpose for their lives by being blinded as to *his* plans for them. Hank knew that a human father's love for a child could be damaging if not given with prayer and the acceptance to allow the Lord to work *his* purpose in their lives.

So in his prayers for these two he so loved, he continued to pray, *Thy will be done, Father, and not my own.* And now he had set the scene, giving them a chance to know one another. They were both too smart for their own good, he thought with tongue in cheek, and they were both comfortable alone in their travels. So he had given instructions for Karl to spend three months learning the music business from Lea. His instructions to Lea was to secretly help Karl recover from his mental wartime wounds he didn't realize he was suffering from because of his highly skilled physicians' training as a medic psychiatrist. "And doctors, especially shrinks, think themselves bulletproof while helping everyone else to cope with stress," he had explained to Lea.

They both would humor his requests because of their love and respect for him and their ingrained discipline as true Christians. So, let them in their unique intelligent minds suspect his old man scheming motives as cupid.

Either way, they would learn to know one another. And God willing, well, miracles happen everyday.

"So is your room here in the hotel?" Lea asked Karl, when the waitress carried away an armful of dishes.

"Yes. In the pool area," he said.

She nodded. "Our production team has been starting early. Most have chosen to stay closer to the showroom making it easier to stay in contact during rehearsal. So you may wish to move closer." Taking a business card from her wallet, Lea jotted down the hotel manager's name and phone number in small exact print on the back.

"The manager can have your luggage brought over to the other room if you wish to make the move. If you need me, my contact numbers are on the card. I may not answer my cell, so dial the office number and leave a message with my secretary, Jerry Handly. He or any office person will take any calls I miss 24/7. I will receive your message and get back to you."

Karl watched her with some questions as to how a twenty-six year old would need a personal secretary and full-time office staff at her disposal twenty-four hours a day. Nonetheless, she spoke of it with such nonchalance it seemed a natural part of her existence.

"So, fine sirs. I will bid you both a good evening. Hank, will we have an early breakfast together?"

"Wish I could, kiddo, but it's time I visited the homestead. My ole dog, Thump, is having a time keeping track of the three kids still at home."

Both men slid out from the booth seat with her. Karl watched his dad bid Lea goodbye. No hug, just a warm handshake, so gentle from his old dad one would think she was some queen stepped off her high seat to honor him. She then left with a simple nod his way.

"Let's sit awhile and have a visit, son, before we hit the sack. How about going over your last few months with me? I lost track of you after your last call. Your e-mails told me you were safe, but I read some conflict between the lines. You seemed angry over the discharge of a patient."

"Angry? Sure, as always, when I realize my limitations. These men deserve so much more help than they get for living through a hell on earth. Then when they're—" Karl rubbed an unsteady hand over his face. "I'm sorry, Dad."

"Why? For letting an old soldier share in his boy's healing process? It doesn't take a PhD in psychiatry for me to understand what you've been through. Do you think I've forgotten how it was? It gets easier with time, but we never forget. A World War II vet told me once that he would never want to live through those war years again, but what he did live through, he would never want to forget.

"The best thing you can do for your patients when you've done all you can do is to give them over to God. Pray for them, son. The Lord cares. They are *his* children. Give them up so you can move forward and help others. Don't lose focus of the importance of your profession. They wouldn't want that. Stay healthy and strong-minded. Heavenly Father will never forget them when they've been beat up and worn down. Remember that story I taught you as a kid about the lump of coal?

What does that common old lump turn into when put under great pressure?"

Hank looked into his boy's eyes, almost too beautiful for a man, and could see the ache there.

"I've tried to focus this last year, Dad, as you taught me. But it's like our Lord is slipping away from me. At times I try to call out to him, and I can't. It's the emptiest feeling I've ever known." Weary, Karl shrugged. "Now I've worried you. How much do you carry on your shoulders, Dad?"

"There was a time I tried to carry it all. Couldn't do it. So I put you and all my loved ones in God's care. I pray for your protection everyday and give thanks that no matter what trials you face, *he* is with you. Psalm 139:1–18 says it better than I ever could. And so I tell myself as I will tonight when I think about you and your doubt that *he* is before you, my boy, and *he* is behind you, around and about you, above and beneath you. He was there with you in the beginning, he is here with you now, and he will be with you when I travel from here and on into eternity. What safer hands could I place you in?

"At times when we doubt our faith, it is a good thing. Our search makes us stronger Christians. Now, get to bed. Even marines need sleep. I'll talk to you in a week or so. Skedaddle."

3

At four in the morning, the one thing that became apparent to Karl was that Las Vegas never slept. At least a few card games continued all night, and the talking slot machines were calling out to him as he passed by. Coffee. The all-night coffee shop would hopefully be quiet. He could hide away there for an hour, walk for two, shower, and be ready for his first day learning his father's "business."

Lea Renton would be an easy female to avoid. As he thought back to the night before, it seemed that she was as uninterested in him as he was in her. She was kindly polite, which he knew was her way, and patient to be sitting through a meal with him, but he knew that her full attention was on his dad. Karl wondered with sudden curiosity just what her attraction was to him. There was a fondness there that was apparent, but what was the reason behind it, and was that attraction shared by his father? Could it be a romantic one?

Impossible! His dad was too much a gentleman to take advantage of a twenty-six year old, no matter how mentally grown-up she was. But perhaps the attraction was on her part?

Just as he stepped into the quiet coffee shop, he spotted the person of his thoughts. And she was sitting at a table face-to-face with an irate Jayson Rawlings. For some reason, seeing the man angry with Lea irritated him, but he took a quieting breath as a sleepy waitress approached him.

"Good morning. You may sit anywhere you wish."

"Thank you. My friends have already arrived," he said.

"Good morning, Karl. Care to join us?" Lea greeted him when he approached their table.

With a curt nod, Jayson welcomed Karl after not seeing him for several years. "Some other time, ole buddy. Not to be rude, but we've a business meeting going on here."

If Jayson was irritated over a disagreement with Lea before, he was totally agitated now. Karl Benson was one that somehow rubbed him the wrong way. He couldn't quite figure out why. Karl was a quiet guy to have around, and one could speak without the man giving his two-cents worth every five minutes. But when he did say something, people listened. Maybe that was the problem. Just a few words from Karl and people listened.

"Great opportunity for me to learn some of the goings on, wouldn't you say so, Ms. Renton?" Karl asked as he pushed in beside Jayson.

"You're very welcome to join in, but the meeting is over," Lea said.

When Jayson opened his mouth to disagree, the waitress appeared to ask Karl if he wanted coffee.

"Please."

Pouring him a cup from the coffee pot she carried with her, she had refilled Jayson's cup when Lea asked for more hot water.

"Do you drink coffee?" Karl asked her.

"Yes. But I limit myself and drink herb tea on the side."

"I could drink ten gallons a day, and it wouldn't bother me in the least." The nervous Jayson smirked.

Karl noticed that Lea hid a grin. It was not much more than a twinkle in her eyes, but when her glance met his, she knew she had been caught. When Karl raised his eyebrows in suspicion, she simply smiled a beautiful smile.

"You're breakfast will be up in a few minutes," the waitress told Lea. She handed her the teapot while asking Karl if he wanted a breakfast menu.

"No need. The morning special will do."

"A man that's easy to please *and* good looking! That's one for the books!" The lady laughed, as she walked away.

"So how does it feel to be back in the states, Doc? Are you totally cut loose from your military obligations?"

"Totally."

"Hank says you're taking a break from your medical practice. You giving it up for good?"

"I haven't decided."

Jayson grunted. "Seems like an expensive load of education flushed down the toilet."

Karl gave him a cool stare.

"Nothing we learn is wasted," Lea commented.

"Is that so?" Jayson said rudely. "Explain."

"If a doctor's medical studies should help *only* one patient in that doctor's lifetime, is that not worth all his time and expense to have achieved that knowledge?"

Jayson laughed. "Okay. Take all that money and time and put it into a hospital in say—South America or India or Africa. Wouldn't that help so many more than one patient?"

Lea's eyes drifted off into some faraway place. "That is the age-old question, is it not? Is one life worth the many?" she said softly, barely loud enough for both men to hear. Karl stared as if he had never seen her before.

The waitress leaned over the table, balancing a heaping tray of breakfast food on her arm. "Granola and fresh fruit with yogurt, my dear." She set them neatly before Lea. "You sir, your ham omelet with hash browns. And your order, blue eyes, will be right up. More coffee, anyone?"

"Sure," Jayson nodded. He dug into his meal with gusto. Lea seemed to enjoy watching him eat. He put so much of himself into everything he did, and Karl had to admit, he was entertaining.

Lea was pouring milk over the bowl of grainy granola cereal when Karl asked, "So outline this business meeting you two were so intense about when I walked in."

"No need, pal. No time to explain," Jayson said.

Lea took a bite of her cereal curious as to how Karl would handle Jayson's obvious rudeness.

"I've watched Hank deal with his agent for some years now," Karl said, "and I find that there's not much to the music business. It's like any other. An online course should get me up to date on the dynamics end of it."

It took all Lea's years in the practice of self-control to keep a blank face when Jayson looked at her with an expression of total exasperation. She took a dainty spoonful of granola into her mouth and chewed slowly, watching his skin turn from a sickly white to a bright red. Just why Jayson had not had a heart attack as yet was beyond her. Just as he opened his mouth to blast his seemingly innocent remark, Karl's breakfast arrived, and the once tired waitress complimented him one too many times on the blueness of his eyes. Jayson had had enough.

"I have a tight schedule so let me out of here!"

"Would you like me to bring you a take-out box to go? You have not finished your meal."

"It is not to my liking, thank you very much!"

"Very well, sir. Have a nice day."

Jayson could only glare at the three of them as Karl scooted over to let him out. "And don't be late," he growled at Lea as he stormed by.

"I hope he's paying you enough, dear," the waitress commented as she reached over to take up Jayson's plate before Karl took his seat again. "Now you two relax and enjoy your breakfast."

"So is he?" Karl asked, scooping up a steaming bite of hash browns.

"So is he what?"

"Paying you enough?"

"Some jobs are not valued in dollars and cents."

Karl took a chance. "In other words, you're doing this job for Hank."

Lea gazed at him for a long moment. "My connection with your father is and always has been in the name of friendship."

Wow. She gets to the point, Karl thought, watching her with interest. This meeting was going great after all.

Karl felt generous. "So. I owe you one, if you wish."

Lea smiled her smile. "You're sure about that?"

Karl frowned. He was a moment ago.

Lea took a sip of her tea, watching him over the rim of the cup as she did so. For the first time in his life, Karl knew what it was like to be one of his own patients.

"Okay then," she said. "Who is to blame when one of your patients does not make it back to reality?"

The coffee that Karl was about to sip never reached his lips. He carefully placed the cup back into its saucer.

"Say again?"

The intense blue of his eyes did not intimidate Lea. She was prepared for the anger there. After all, how would one of his stature in the medical field take to a woman of her age assuming to even dare to step over such a line as this? And who was to blame for the lost? The doctor? The patient? The war? Life? The list went on. And was there an answer? He was the kind of man that would give his mind and heart to each one of his people, and he would not be easy on anyone responsible for letting them down. And of course, he had chosen to place that blame as she knew he would. She could see it in his eyes. Karl watched as her lips asked the question a second time.

"Who is to blame when one of your patients does not make it back to reality?"

It was not pleasant, the smile he gave her. But in his sense of fairness, he had given her permission to ask a question. Well. One question and one question only and that would be the end of it. The clear focus of her eyes held no triumph, only a touch of sadness. She had somehow made it her mission to help him. And she was young. Young people oftentimes thought they could change the world as he once had. She would learn in time as he had learned that life had a way of slapping a man down. *Man? Was he screwed up! He had been thinking of her! Well, he had to give her credit for courage. Now what was the question?*

Gently, she asked once again, "Who is to blame when one of your patients does not make it back to reality?"

Must he say it? "Mine."

Lea sadly shook her head and heard him laugh.

Taking a deep breath, Karl thought, *This is not good! I've lost my cool and now I'll be stuck here listening to some immature diagnosis for the next hour!* But instead she set him back a few steps.

"All right. Your diagnosis," he said through gritted teeth.

"My diagnosis—very well. You think much of yourself."

Karl studied her waiting for more of an explanation, but she began eating her yogurt with calm, dainty spoonfuls. He was going to ignore her, but the process became so irritating he could not help himself. He shook his head and made a conscious effort to calm down.

"Explain."

"Well, Doctor, I see your problem as pride. Pride is one of our most damaging sins. It gets us into more trouble. In fact, it is so terrible the Bible teaches that the Lord *abhors* pride in his children."

Karl caught himself scowling and remembered the look on Jayson's face when he came to the table a short time earlier. To make matters worse, he now felt himself reverting back to his childhood sarcasm and thought, *So, now she's a Bible scholar!*

"And just how, Ms. Doctor Renton, do you see me as proud?"

Lea calmly set her spoon down. "Well, you see, it is the patient's choice to return to reality. Not yours. Now when you think that you are in control of a person's life, you are trying to take away that person's God-given right of choice. To even dare to think that you can decide what is best for a child of God is ridiculous. He has given that child the right of choice for a reason. You, Karl Benton, are *not* and can *never* be God, and I will presume that you would never *want* to be God. So, if you are only a man, how can it be your responsibility that your patient does not make it back to reality if it is his choice not to do so? Is that not beyond your control? Could pride be causing the confusion here?

"So, I clearly see pride as the cause of your reasoning in this case. And because I struggle with the same sin, as we all do, I can recognize it. You see, I am at the advantage of standing from a distance. Therefore, I can pinpoint the problem. You cannot because of your involvement with your patient."

Lea paused. When Karl only stared at her, she said, "And now if you'll excuse me, I'm running late. By the way, your meal is paid for," she added, snatching up the three breakfast tabs as she stood.

Karl watched her pay the cashier and disappear through the doorway before realizing that he was painfully gritting his teeth.

⁂

The large bottled water that Karl had purchased that morning after leaving the coffee shop was two-thirds used up. With the sun beating down on him, his white sweat-soaked T-shirt had a familiar feel to it as it clung to his back and chest. And with a dry mouth and sinuses burning, the drive into the foothills west of the town for a grueling workout proved a good decision.

The city limits had taken some time to reach with boulevards, morning traffic, and stoplights to navigate. The restrictions of city life were making him feel squeezed in until he found the open desert, much to his relief.

An hour now had passed on foot, and he was as far into the foothills as he should go. No one knew where he was, and the area was isolated with loose rock that could throw him easily off balance at his pace. With no fear of snakes, he still respected them. He would stay alert especially around shady areas and brush where the rattlesnakes of the Mojave Desert were fond of resting.

The welcome exercise helped to ease the tension he had felt since driving into the busy Las Vegas town the night before and especially since his therapy session with the woman his dad had sent to "help" him. He laughed without humor. No more in-depth conversations with her! The few women he knew were comfortable enough to talk with, but this female had a way of setting him off-balance. He did not need any more amateur psychotherapy sessions of hers screwing him up anymore than he already was.

Pride? *pride*? The word kept setting him off again and again. How could one little bit of fluff upset his whole morning as she had? And that wily waitress asking him if he wanted a take-out box? Renton would not ruin his appetite! Even if he had to choke the whole breakfast down! Every last particle! And he couldn't even pay for his own meal! She had taken care of feeding him! The thought of leaving twenty dollars on the table to spite her was impossible. That wild waitress lady might get the wrong idea and think it was her tip. And chances were he would have to eat there again on her watch.

Karl finally slowed to a walk. It was time to start back to town. He hiked up a steep slope, kicking sandy peddles loose as he reached the top and squatted down to rest. From there, the valley was as brown as the eye could see, and the dry sandy smell of clean, sun-bleached sand and sage brush felt good in his lungs.

The intense morning sun made him glad for his dark glasses as he wondered what his squad was up to at the moment. *Conley and Danner. Those two characters! They had only months left of duty before heading back to the States. Would they make it home?* The sweat dripping down his back suddenly felt icy cold. The whole bunch appeared to be so tough, as all marines did, but deep down one could feel the reality of death so keenly. At one moment a man could be laughing quietly with a buddy, the next begging his friend's heart to keep beating—just a little longer. The ache came again. That deep, gut-wrenching ache! He hid his face in his hands needing so badly to weep, but the tears just wouldn't come.

Tired now, Karl forced himself to stand and began the decent step by step. War. That metallic scent of war. He could still smell it. Picking up his step, he thought of the guys. They joked about him being a shrink. Seldom had he worked in a hospital setting unless called in. He requested to be on the line with the men where he would be needed the most in and after a battle. Most of the time he was a regular marine soldier—like a field Chaplin there to counsel when needed during a skirmish or after a random bombing that took them by surprise. The dead…The dead were easy compared to the wounded! His heart still ached for the wounded…

At first he had felt like he made a difference, but as the men needed him more and more for support, the war got more and more ugly. When one lived with those he was responsible for, they became closer than patients. They became like the brothers he never had as a kid.

Being a kid was like a dark dream. He was twelve years old when Hank found him in the home. Being able to handle only one child at the time, Hank had to choose, and he chose him, a quiet, angry boy too world-wise for his own good. But as new as Hank was at the game, he had enough love in his giant heart to somehow make him a natural at the "dad" job.

Hank had a million crazy ways to entertain a kid. It began with his Wild West songs one summer night on the front porch of his Texas ranch home. He got one of his ancient, worn-out cow dogs howling to his tunes, making a cranky kid finally crack a smile. Then, from somewhere deep down inside, that kid learned that night how to laugh. And it began with Hank twanging ridiculously on his guitar while singing with his sidekick cook and wrangler Snoop, teaching a lonely boy at twelve years of age how to laugh aloud. The sound was as strange a sound at first in his ears as it felt coming out from inside of him. But that scruffy old toothless dog sitting beside those two goofy cowboys howling like he was part of the band, just grabbed him up that night from some lonely place he had been stuck in all his life.

Little by little, Hank taught him the presence of his Lord. Hank introduced him to the Holy Spirit, and he had truly never been alone since. But then in the last couple of years, some of that loneliness had seeped back inside of him. Yes, it has a name—fear. It is the fear of one's mortality. The loss of faith in the power of the Creator. It is the loss of hope. The discomfort is staggering. The need to regain the confidence in his faith was becoming a yearning, but it seemed always, just out of reach. Still, he was a man of prayer and thankfulness as his dad taught him, and the quiet, familiar voice kept his whisper of encouragement, *"I'll never leave you. You are mine."*

Karl pulled the plastic bottle from inside his sweaty T-shirt and finished the now tepid water. It was time to focus on the days ahead. Soon, hopefully, he'd be accepted as part of the fixtures, like a fly on the wall; and perhaps he could sleep the days away in one of the thousands of padded showroom chairs. After all, if he could sit in a foxhole for forty-eight hours in 100 degree temperatures with snipers bearing down on him, he could be wined and dined for a week or more, sleep in a feathered bed, lounge by a pool under the excellent care of the hotel's refreshment team, and gaze upon beautiful dancers while dreaming of being one day closer to the end of the elegant entertaining hell of so-called luxury living.

4

Karl had been living the "easy" life for several days now with no word from his dad. While trying to stir an interest within himself in the workings of the entertainment industry, he watched Lea work with her team while noticing that some of the well-known performers knew her personally. She was an accomplished song writer and made an enormous living on that alone, but he learned that her family was wealthy and she had no need to work if she did not choose to. But work she did and somehow made it look easy.

After knowing her for only a short time, Karl learned that Lea's youth was overlooked because of her own disregard of it. She was an "ageless" person, and he guessed she would be until the day she died. She had an inner kindness but was no pushover. Men and women alike respected her as she respected them. The more he came to know her, the more he thought her not of the world she lived in. And he was determined to learn of her, from her birth to the present day.

This day had been a long one. As he watched the process of fine-tuning the musical part of the production for opening night on the Las Vegas strip, Karl could not help but find it interesting. There were billboards advertising the opening, and people spoke of the "night" in excited whispers. The excitement was there when he arrived, but he had overlooked it as he thought of it as an artificial part of the town. Now he began to look deeper as to how the success of *Summer's Night* would affect so many peoples' lives. Las Vegas created work for many, thus creating financial security for families from restaurant cooks, waitresses, and staff; hotel personnel, gardeners; also, government workers, and others, not to mention people like Jayson whose career was on the line if the "night" would prove a failure.

As evening settled into dinnertime once again, and Lea was seated with Karl and Jayson in the elegant hotel dining room, the ever watchful Karl noticed Jayson's interest in a customer's complaints concerning his meal. The formal dining room's chef was as meticulous as they came, but still the man was not happy.

"Why does that waitress take that? I'd tell him to cook his own dinner, or is that why he's eating out?" Jayson said.

Lea watched the waitress as she carried the steaming plate of food back towards the kitchen. "Some of us will put up with much to keep our positions."

"What's this 'us' all about?" Jayson snorted. "You have no need to keep a job. You could tell me anytime to 'take this job and shove it!'"

"How's that?" Karl asked around a strawberry he had popped into his mouth from the fruit bowl that came with his dinner.

Jayson gave Karl his familiar smirk. "Well. Since you're a country usually unheard from, Mr. 'Don't Get Involved Doctor Guy,' she's richer than Moses's Pharaoh. She doesn't know what needing to make a buck means."

"You seem to measure work in monetary value, Jayson," Lea said.

"Alright. So why are you putting up with my crap? Or do you secretly enjoy it?" Jayson challenged.

Lea shook her head.

"What? Playing Mother Teresa again, Ms. Holy? So. No preaching this evening? Am I one of the lost lambies? The one that fell over the cliff and Shepherd Boy was secretly filled with joy to be rid of me?"

"You seem to think I don't like you, Jayson," she said, thoughtfully. "When have I given you that impression?"

"Come on, kid! Who in their right mind would enjoy being anywhere within ten feet of me? Even in church, there seems to be an invisible wall wherever I find myself. Reminds me of the leper stories in the Bible."

Lea touched the condensed moisture on her water glass, then studied the tips of her fingers where the drops reflected light from the lamp hanging over the table. "You're wrong if you think I don't like being around you."

Jayson made a face. "Are you trying to tell me that crudeness does not annoy someone like you?"

"I'm not agreeing with you if you're referring to yourself as 'crude.' And I'm not a stranger to 'crude,' Jayson. There is one thing that I can assure you—a Mother Teresa I certainly am not."

Both men watched her, questions very apparent left hanging in the air. But Lea was finished with that part of the conversation and was very apt at changing the subject.

Later that evening as he lay upon the starched hotel sheets, Karl could not get her admission from his mind—"A Mother Teresa I certainly am not." *Wow! What an insight as to how she saw herself. She did work around worldly men and women, so she had to be familiar with inappropriate language and behavior from some of them. And Dad was right about her maturity. She was without a doubt aged beyond her years.*

Karl took a deep breath and exhaled in the silence of the dark hotel room. "Lea Ann Renton? Who are you?" he whispered, as he drifted off to sleep.

5

Lea stood on center stage, one hand on a hip, the other held a clipboard. She had taken off her suit jacket and wore a white long-sleeved shirt rolled up above the elbows. The shirt was tucked neatly into her usual dark slacks. With feet slightly apart, her black no-nonsense non-feminine shoes were balanced securely upon the polished wooden floor. She could have been a slender young man instructing a group of musicians, except for her very feminine shape and grace.

"Alright! We're closing up shop for two hours. Remember the drill. Two things will not be tolerated. One is excess alcohol. The second is showing up late. See you all back here at two-thirty. Stay in the hotel area."

"Lee! I'd like to stay and practice awhile—"

"No deal, Michael!" she called out to a young man sitting at his keyboard. "Your instructions are to eat lunch and rest."

Jayson shouted up at her to be heard over the murmur of the group. "Hey, Lee! I'm calling a meeting in ten minutes in the conference room. Be there!"

Sarah, who was passing by, looked startled. "What will you be needing from—"

"I need to run a couple things by Renton. Take a break!"

Ten minutes later, Lea stood at a window in the conference room gazing down upon a soothing view of green grass, palm trees, and blue ponds of water when Jayson literally crashed through the door. Immediately, Karl came in behind him, earning a scowl. It was a large office Jayson rented to serve as a meeting place with anyone he wanted to impress.

"You don't have to be here, Benson."

"We have no secrets from Karl." She turned to face them.

"You've been acting like he's your hired body guard—or is it—"

"Just stop or this meeting is finished."

Jayson seemed taken back. Lea had never been sharp with him before, and this was bordering on rudeness. And he was no child to be put in his place.

"I don't take crap from my employees, no matter who they are."

"I am not one of your employees, Jayson."

"So! There it is, isn't it? No contract. No discussion on pay. You are your own boss."

"My reasons for working with you are my own business."

Jayson had not seen Lea angry before. And one could not really call it anger. She simply did not let him push her around.

"Yea. It would be nice to be one's own person." He watched her, Karl's presence forgotten where he sat off to one side of the room. "I guess if one is rich enough they can afford to have no one to answer to."

Lea looked down to study her favorite silver pen she held in one hand. "Everyone has someone to answer to, Jayson."

"So you're talking God again."

She reached up to slide the pen above her ear as she walked to a chair and sat down. "Not necessarily."

"So, Renton. Who is your boss?"

She couldn't help it. Her slow smile gentled her lips as he had a way of amusing her. "Why am I here this afternoon? Is there a problem?"

Jayson paced the floor before her. "Okay, I need to know where I stand. We've opening night coming up in two days, and I need a guarantee that you'll be there. I get the feeling that you're ready to run out on me."

Lea bowed her head and closed her eyes. She then looked up and studied the man standing before her for a long moment. "I cannot make a promise I might not be able to keep. I will try my best to be here on opening night."

"How do I live with that? What if I need you to step in, say, the drummer gets sick or the pianist. I've no backups that know the complete program as you do."

"Jayson. It's just like life. There are no guarantees. But if something should go wrong, it won't be the end of the world. If I cannot be here for some reason and something goes wrong, there are other musicians on call that are very able to step in and do the job."

"No one can do the job as you can. I've seen you stand in during rehearsals and your work with individuals in off-time hours. You've got it all down and then some—"

"Jayson. I do not make promises. And after opening night, I'm flying out."

He turned pale, for once having nothing to say.

Lea stood. She was tall enough to face him at eye level. She then said very quietly, "You know your work, Jayson. You won't need me after Friday night."

❧

Hank and Karl stood outside in the warm night air watching as people filed out of the elegant showroom, the excitement of the audience a clear indication that *Summer's Night* would be playing for a long time to come. Lea's job was finished; and as she promised Jayson, her plans were to be at the airport within the hour. She had said her goodbyes to her team the evening before at an informal dinner in one of the huge buffet rooms of the hotel.

Friends were waiting nearby for Hank to join up with after the two men said their goodbyes. Lea would meet Karl in the hotel lobby by the valet desk. Their luggage was waiting in baggage claim and would be carried to her rental car. He had given his car up to the rental agency the day before. Both Lea and Karl were used to travel and were comfortable with it. Both could sleep just about anywhere. Both were quiet people, easy to please. They would travel well together. It was time to move on.

6

Lea taxied her jet into position on the runway, engines humming. Ground control gave permission for takeoff. The power of liftoff always gave Lea a sense of freedom. She handled very well the stress of being needed by so many, or as she knew, Holy Spirit gave her the mind and heart to help so many of his children in need. But still, she was only a human being in body, and even hers needed rest from time to time, so she had learned long ago not to feel guilty for doing so.

My thanks to you, Heavenly Father, Lord Jesus, Holy Spirit. I leave these children in your care as always. Shaking loose her concern for Jayson, Sarah, and so many others she had been working with, Lea was already looking ahead.

"My thanks to *you*, my God, for thy many blessings in my life," she whispered as the power of the small but superb aircraft's wheels gripped the asphalt runway and then lifted off into the familiar weightless climb.

It was a beautiful machine. One she literally entrusted her life to, and tonight, the life of her passenger. As she studied the technical lights of the instrument panel in the darkness of the cockpit, she felt quite relaxed. Her hours in control of her plane even surpassed her hours driving behind the wheel of an automobile.

The man sitting beside her in the copilot seat was as quiet as she. Lea could tell by his posture that he was not anxious with her in control of the jet. She knew he had watched her every move before relaxing onto the seat—before leaving his life in her hands. Confidence, the efficiency of procedure, quality of the machine, all that he had observed as she knew he would, had been satisfactory to him. He was a marine, a soldier accustomed to danger, but he was also no fool regarding human life.

Lea had been a well-accomplished pilot for years. Necessity of air travel did not take away her love of it, but then again, her love of it never made her sloppy. She appreciated the gift given her and was very professional in her responsibilities. She knew that being confident as a child of God did not give her permission to act irresponsibly and test her Lord's patience.

She was thirsty but would wait until altitude was reached before concerning herself with personal comfort. They were still within multiple travel patterns of aircraft coming and going from the Las Vegas airport. This to her was one of the critical areas of flying, when close to a busy airfield. Soon they would be in their own spacious air highway high above the ground.

Lea sensed the man beside her as he glanced her way. "How are you?" she asked.

Karl gave her a thumbs-up and continued his watch of the sky.

Air highway, she thought. How she loved to teach children about flying—to put the technology into words that they understood. And as Jesus taught in parables, she taught children in the same way. They loved stories that caught their interest of the valuable life lessons to be learned and in turn the stories made learning fun. She missed being around children these past months. So many adults had needed her lately, and it was her music that provided the necessary escape she needed. It was an enjoyable challenge, and one she loved so much—her music.

"I will sing our new song with you, Lord, in thought," she whispered quietly:

Lord, I forget how to pray
Only you ease my way
Teach me not to turn away
Lord, I forget how to pray…

Lord, I forget how to cry
Tears clear fear from my eyes
Wash away this pain of mine
Lord, I forget how to cry…

Lord, I forget how to love
Gentle me like the dove
Fill my mind with love divine
Lord, I forget how to love
Lord, I forget how to love…

Lea whispered, "How simple, and yet not. *Simplicity*—even the word is lovely!" As she studied the air traffic's blinking lights all about her, talking silently with Holy Spirit, Karl was not totally forgotten. During the short time she had known him, she had learned from necessity to be comfortable in his presence. He was a man that could take a woman's energy, and she could not allow that to happen. For Hank's sake, and for his, she would relax around him, be herself, accept him as a friend, and God willing, be her Lord's instrument in helping him.

From what Hank had told her, and from what she had been praying to understand, she hoped she could be the helper he needed at this time in his life. Not that she was anyone special. Still, she could be her Lord's messenger. Karl was a child of Heavenly Father, and she had been called to be a friend to him. That was what she would be.

7

The lights of the runway were a homecoming to Lea. Grandfather knew that she was on her way home with a friend. Karl would hardly be the first. So many times through the years she had brought them home. Mostly it was women or the young that needed a break from family problems, or a helping hand with their music studies. This friend would be a surprise to him.

It was usually late, and the ancient clock standing in the large hallway of the house would be chiming the early morning hours when Lea would arrive home with her students. Grandfather's old-time companion, Jacob, welcomed home the travelers, sending them up to the old man's room for a cup of his favorite herbal tea. "It helps one to sleep, especially after a long night of travel," was his medical advice. And as Lea usually slept well when home with Grandfather, she wondered if his old fashioned remedy had some truth to it.

The small private airfield's lights were left on mostly for her now, as Grandfather did not fly back and forth to his work as in his younger days. Though he did fly, as it was a very special pleasure in life, he worked mostly from his home office now, needing to stay in control of his own business interests. At eighty-two years of age, Philip Renton was clear of mind and suffered with only the common aches and pains of his age group. And if cocky feistiness could be a cure for old age, he had his share of it.

If Lea had taken after anyone in her family, it would be her Grandfather Philip in his cool business sense. But that was where the similarity stopped and her grandmother's gentleness began. Philip always said that she had so much of his beautiful Janie in her; he never missed his marriage of fifty-one years when Lea was home from her "wanderings."

There was a bond between grandfather and granddaughter that was strong. They almost knew one another's thoughts; and as their unique intimacy was so noticeable even of the stranger within the family gatherings, it made for some difficulties for Lea within her mother's siblings' group. Most of them worried over Grandfather's favoritism of Lea. Not only because of her keen mind, but especially because of the comparison in looks and temperament to her cherished grandmother that made her clearly Grandfather's favorite. And because of his abundant wealth, well, of course wealth could cause one grief at times with worry over being left out in the end.

Now Lea was not at all covetous with monetary things, and in her generosity it seemed to be abundantly given to her in return. But the family members could not see her in that light, seeing her only as a threat to their future. And Grandfather did include only Lea in his business ventures. Even though she was prone to being too generous and trusting, he also knew her to be no one's fool. The trusting part of her was so much his Janie, he allowed her to work on his unbelief as he had allowed her grandmother. And he loved her for it, thinking perhaps in the end the efforts of the two women of his life would get him into heaven, a belief that made Lea's heart ache, for after all, "only Jesus Christ is the way to a heavenly future."

Yes, Lea was not at all covetous with wealth and was careful not to flaunt it in any way, sharing it by helping others as she believed it to be given her to do with. In return, as much as she gave, she received through not only her grandfather's business ventures that he asked her to partner him with, but her own; she in turn loved, trusted, and obeyed him even as to letting him become involved in her own songwriting talents. Though she wrote and sold under another name, still, many knew of her and asked her to help their groups in inspiring them to succeed. And so, with Grandfather Philip's blessing, and because he knew her heart so well, he encouraged her to be the teacher to young musicians and troubled youths as she felt called to be. She was so much like his Janie, he knew of her needs.

Lea knew that her new focus was much more of an in-depth project than the youth she normally worked with and was not sure as to how Grandfather would greet her newest friend. So she would be as always, very open with him. Hopefully, Grandfather would agree to meet him the next day, after she had time to present Karl's introduction in a timelier manner.

"Lea Ann! It's too late for children to be out and about. You should be getting your beauty sleep. Well—perhaps not. You just get prettier."

"Jacob. You do my old heart good," Lea said with a laugh. But it was at that moment she had a preview of her grandfather's reaction to Karl's presence. As he stepped into the doorway behind her, suitcases in hand, she thought again that perhaps she should have prepared the way for her "newest" friend.

"Jacob, this is Karl Benson. He will be working and traveling with me for a few months. Karl, Jacob is, well, Jacob is family."

"It's good to meet you, sir," Karl said. He set the suitcases down to take the older man's hand in his big, firm, but careful handshake. It warmed Lea's heart to see him treat the old gentleman with such respect, and in return Jacob warmed to him instantly.

"And it is a pleasure to meet you, son. Phil knows you kids are here, so if you will have your visit before you settle in, he just may get some sleep yet tonight."

Jacob grinned up at Karl since the younger man was so much taller in height. "You see, when his girl starts for home, Phil's like a kid waiting for Christmas morning."

Lea sighed. *How should she explain Karl's presence to Grandfather?* While hesitating, pondering her situation, both Jacob and Karl sensed her confusion.

"Jacob?" she asked.

"Yes?"

"Jacob, perhaps it would be best if Karl meet Grandfather in the morning."

The old man stared at her for a few moments before understanding her dilemma.

"Yes. Yes! I will show him to his rooms. You go on up and have your visit. Son, you come with me, and I'll get you comfortable for a good rest."

Lea looked at Karl, away, and back again. He was so astute! Here was no youth she was dealing with.

She felt irritated at the warmth that filled her cheeks, sensing the laughter in his expression. *How long had it been since she had not been able to laugh at herself?*

With a frown, she left him with the very capable Jacob and trotted up the staircase feeling both men's eyes upon her, until disappearing behind her grandfather's door.

8

Lea found him sitting in his favorite chair before the hearth that in the summer months had a light inside, giving off a feeling of coziness.

"Grandfather! I've missed you."

Kneeling beside him to rest her head against his chest, the warmth of his arms and strong, familiar beat of his heart was always a balm to her fatigue upon coming home. Only he knew how weary she could become and how well she hid it even from herself.

He held her back from him for a few moments to study her face. "So, are you looking ahead as you know you must? Are you leaving your flock behind?"

Lea nodded, her eyes taking in the age of his beloved face. He smelled of his old-time spicy aftershave. His thinning hair was combed back neatly, and he was as always clean shaven. Philip Renton was a proper gentleman to his very bones, a businessman. Business had been his life's work, and he loved its ongoing, demanding pace.

She knew that he would not ready himself for sleep until she was safely tucked into her room for the night. His attire even at this hour was almost formal.

He was fully dressed except for the comfortable evening jacket he wore in place of his suit jacket. The handsome jacket had been a Christmas gift from her. Every other year she gave him a new one, wrapped in a box of gold-and-white striped foil paper and adorned with a wide golden bow. The family had learned that any jacket, no matter how grand, would be politely acknowledged, put into his closet for a few months, and then passed on to a needy gentleman in the town's retirement home.

"Yes. You have my assurance that I have left my 'flock' in Holy Spirit's care."

"As you do with me when you fly away into the clouds?"

"Always, Grandfather," she said softly, willing her eyes to stay clear of the tears she always felt when leaving him, and even now with just the thought of leaving him once again. Pulling her favorite foot stool from before her grandmother's chair, she placed it beside his knee. There she could rest lightly against him. Ignoring the new signs of age showing on his handsome features since her short absence, she jumped ahead to the present. Too precious was he for her to contemplate the day when he would complete his work in this present life, and she would have to let him go.

"So. Is our newest business adventure keeping you as busy as we predicted?"

"We had no doubt." He grinned, too cocky for his own good.

With a slow deep breath, Lea gazed at him knowingly. "I will check with Jacob on just how busy we're talking about."

"He knows enough to mind his own business. Now to yours. This new friend. Tell me about her. Or is this a child you have brought home?"

Blue-green eyes peered into soft-brown. He knew her so well.

"I'm helping a friend's son, Grandfather."

"Ah!"

They had had this conversation before.

"He is a friend, sir"

"I will meet him now."

Lea looked down to remove a small speck of lint from her slacks. She had mishandled Karl's introduction by not leaving him to follow.

Lord! What shall I do? she implored. And the words came quietly clear, *Obey.*

As she went in search of Karl, Lea thought back to the last time she had brought home a man to "help." She was young. They worked in her studio that Grandfather built for her after she came to live with him. It was after her mother and father were killed in an automobile accident on a New Year's Eve night.

Lea had come from her home in New York City to live with her grandparents in Sun Valley, Idaho a year after the accident. It took several months before Grandfather built her a recording studio of her own on his estate at the request of his wife, who thought the sun rose and set for her Lea Ann. Then at eighteen years of age Lea brought home a young man as one of her "students." As intelligent as she was in most things, her trust in people did not prepare her for learning of the man's true nature. But she was taught a valuable lesson. One she would never forget, nor would her grandfather…

Jacob now met Lea at the bottom of the stairs. "Karl is settled in the guest rooms. He does not wish to eat, so I left him some things in case he gets hungry before breakfast time—What has happened, child?"

"I must ask Karl to have a talk with Grandfather."

"I'll fetch him for you."

"Thank you, Jacob."

Lea sat on a wide step at the bottom of the staircase. It was lovely with a curved railing that any child would of course dare to slide down. She had done it only once and was caught by her grandmother, who had been so frightened that she could have fallen from the height of it, Lea had never done it again.

How tired she felt! Leaning her head upon her knees, she thought about what it would mean to disobey her grandfather and choose to obey Holy Spirit's wishes to help Karl. It would break Grandfather's heart for her to put him second in her list of priorities. *Please Lord; don't let it come to that! Nevertheless, thy will be done—*

Karl and Jacob stood for several moments watching her, head resting upon her knees where she sat at the bottom of the staircase.

"Lea."

Karl had called to her. *Had she been asleep?*

"Excuse me." Lea stood supporting herself with one hand on the railing. "Karl, Grandfather wishes to see you."

"That's fine. Perhaps you may wish to get some sleep? Jacob can show me the way."

The tiredness was so intense, she nodded. "Yes. Thank you."

"I'll take good care of him, Lea Ann," Jacob assured her.

She nodded. "Goodnight then."

9

Lea awoke to a quiet house. How long had she slept? Daylight peaked through the cracks of the blinds on her bedroom windows. Having closed her eyes to starlight shining through, Juanita, the hardworking little housekeeper, must have checked on her before the morning sun came up and closed the blinds so she could sleep. She glanced at the bedside clock glowing in the darkness of her room. *Four o'clock in the afternoon! How could that be?*

Always first to her prayers upon awakening, Lea was quick to shower, dress, and neaten her room. After finding Grandfather's downstairs office empty, she went to the guest room and knocked firmly upon the door. There was no answer, so she opened it a few inches calling out Karl's name before stepping inside.

The spacious sitting room with cream colored sofa and matching chairs were new since she last noticed. There was an attractive coffee table before them with an arrangement of magazines neatly fanned out in its center. There was no sign that anything had been disturbed.

"Karl?"

Knowing him, he probably used the bedroom and bath area, leaving the rest of the place unused, but after checking she found no sign of his things.

"Ms. Lea?"

"Juanita. How are you?" she greeted the little dark-haired woman who lived in the grounds keeper's cottage with her husband and two grandchildren. Juanita always brightened Lea's homecomings.

"Your granddad took the plane this morning with your friend and Mr. Jacob. He give you this." The little housekeeper held out a small envelope.

The note in her grandfather's writing simply said that they would return by bedtime.

"Thank you. How are Miguel and the children?"

"Miguel is good. Jenny say school is fun! Carol do not like it." Juanita shook her head sadly.

"Would you like me to speak with her? Perhaps I could find out if there is a problem?"

"Oh yes! Please, Ms. Lea! She will listen if it be you."

"All right. I will go now."

The clock was chiming seven o'clock before the call came in from Karl. He was in Denver, Colorado and planned to meet up with friends in the morning. Karl was undecided as to his plans after that. Lea couldn't tell what he was feeling about being dismissed by her grandfather, but she would not push him for details. After a polite goodbye and thank you, the call was ended.

Lea knew that Karl's interest in his own father's business was given out of respect. And in turn she counted his loyalty a big plus in character. But if she detected a sense of relief in his tone for being let off-the-hook concerning his commitment, he was sadly mistaken. She had promises to keep and began immediately to pack her bags. But before she could fly out once again, she would have no choice but to face her grandfather.

"Ms. Lea? Please eat your dinner now. It will soon no be good."

"Yes, Juanita. Thank you."

It was a lonely meal, and she had no appetite but ate in respect of Juanita's efforts. At eight-thirty, there was still no sign of her grandfather's plane. Just when she decided to begin an inquiry as to the time of his and Jacob's departure from the Denver airfield, she spotted the aircraft's lights from an upstairs window.

As the two men drove in, she was there at the front door to greet them. Jacob looked weary from his day. He was not fond of flying, and she suspected he had done a good deal of worrying over his promise to her the night before to care for Karl. And Grandfather's face was set in his "don't mess with me, little girl" look that she knew, oh so well!

"Juanita has your dinner waiting, though she's worried it may be a little overdone."

"Very well."

The two men ate quietly while Lea snacked on a home-baked bread roll. Her bags had been noticed sitting by the door. After dinner, Jacob gave her a wink and firm hug before leaving the two of them alone with their coffee.

"I see you've decided to fly out tonight to follow after this marine."

"I've made a commitment, Grandfather."

"To whom?"

"To my Lord and Savior, sir."

"What of your grandfather's wishes? If I should ask you to let this man go, what would you say? He is a soldier home from a war. He's a man who has been without a woman for years, or worse yet, what women may he have been with? He's a man with a man's needs. He's a man of the mind. How many ways can a man like him have to fool a young, vulnerable woman? To trip you up? You don't know the trouble a man like this can cause you."

"I'm no longer a young girl, Grandfather. I am no longer blindly trusting of men, especially smart, handsome men."

"So! You're saying he is smart and handsome!"

Lea took a slow, deep breath. That certainly was not smart on her part! "Yes, he is those things—it is quite obvious. And he is quite well-off financially," she added, knowing better than to acknowledge her grandfather's surprise in anyway.

"Grandfather. I don't know him. That I will admit. But I know of his reputation, and I am safe with him. He will protect me on the road. And we will be traveling sometimes by car. I know how much it worries you when I road travel."

"If I asked you not to see him again?"

And here it was, *the choice*.

10

Denver, Colorado was not a small city; nevertheless, Jacob had given her enough information for Lea to find the hotel where Karl was staying with no trouble. It was very early morning, and she had checked into a room, showered and changed into fresh clothing. Unable to sleep, and knowing Karl's habits, she now sat in the hotel coffee shop. He would surely be coming through the door looking for coffee and an early breakfast.

Knowing of security procedure, Lea knew better than to ask the desk clerk to call up to his room. So she had reading material and settled back with her granola and first cup of coffee for company. But a weary mood also accompanied her, and she knew that some sleep would soon be needed.

The memory of leaving her grandfather made her sad. She had prayed for his understanding, leaving him in Holy Spirit's care as always upon any departure from the beautiful Idaho valley. She loved the place. The warm greens of the summer months were a lazy and sleepy time. Next came fall with its oranges, yellows, and browns. Then fell winter shades of white blanketing the mountainsides with its cool, clean warmth, and finally, finally springtime! Spring…the months of hope, of new beginnings, warmth of sun, melting snow, flowers, and colors unimaginable!

"How are you, Miss? May I warm your coffee?"

Lea blinked up, focusing upon a bashful male waiter who held a pot of steaming coffee.

"Yes, thank you." She watched him carefully refill her cup. His very shyness warmed her to him. "So, do you always work the night shift?"

"I have this summer. I'm starting my junior year at our college soon. Then I'll work on the weekends. The day shift."

"That must be tough, attending college and supporting yourself as you study."

"Yea. Get's rough. For each hour of class time, there is a lot of home study. And then with the cost of tuition and books, it gets expensive. I have a sister who just graduated. Mom and Dad helped some, but Sis worked as much as possible. Did some on student loans, but I'm trying not to. It will just take longer. At least I'm close enough to the university to live at home. Not like some others I know."

"What are you studying?"

"Veterinary medicine. Farm animals."

"Really?"

The boy brightened at Lea's interest but some customers demanded his attention, and he excused himself. It was now five-thirty, and she wondered if Karl would be showing up at all. As much as she did not want to make the call to Hank and worry him, it might become necessary. Another half-hour and she would go to her room to make the call. One way or the other, she would find him.

❧

She found him by the lake. If the place were described, it would be in colors as dabbed upon God's paint board: every blue of the lake and sky, green of the trees and plant life, rich browns of the earth.

He was fishing. No. He had planned to fish but was sitting with his back resting against a log, his fishing gear arranged in a neat pile before him. Lea knew he was aware of her presence. She watched his back waiting until he spoke.

"What are you doing here?"

Lea studied him for a long moment. He was angry. She did not know what to expect when invading his privacy but was not given a choice. He chose not to carry a cell phone, and the cabin did not have a phone of any kind. "I have come to continue our three month's on your study, as your father requested."

When she walked around the fallen log to face him, he sat rudely studying her from head to toe. She was dressed as meticulously tailored and spotless as usual. She had spoken to him in her easy way of getting to the point. She was patient. She was watchful. She was amazingly beautiful. All was the same. *No. All was not the same. There was something different. It was—a kind of weariness.*

"Did your Grandfather give his permission for you to be with me?" he asked.

"Excuse me?"

"Did your Grandfather give his permission for you to be with me?"

Her smile! That smile. It said so much. It said it all. "If you wish to study here, I can call my band in, or we can have a more quiet study."

"*Your* band?" he said with raised brows.

"It is up to you. I'll meet you at the cabin. Will it be fish for dinner, or should I order out?"

"Who invited you to dinner?"

That smile again! "By the way, how did you know it was me?"

"I could smell you."

"Wow. You're good. See ya."

Two hours later, Karl threw three lake trout in the sink, a thin rope still looped through their gills. He was surprised when Lea spread some clean newspaper she found in the trash container out on the counter, slid the fish off the stringer onto it, and slit each belly open with a small sharp knife that he himself preferred for the job. She pulled the intestines out onto the newspaper, then held each fish under the running water gently scraping the knife blade back and forth over the skin to remove the scales. Finally, she held open the slit in each belly to gently rinse and clean the inside with her thumbnail to remove the thick blood vein that ran along the inner spine. After placing them on paper towels layered out upon the scarred linoleum counter top, she quickly rolled up the fish guts inside the newspaper and placed them in a bucket marked TO BEAR CONTAINER. A heavy iron skillet was found in a bottom cupboard and placed upon the biggest burner on the propane fuelled stove top. In the doorless cupboards above the sink, she rummaged around pulling out a salt shaker and bottle of olive oil. Inside the small freezer was found a miniature bag of flour and box of cornmeal.

Next she rolled out a piece of waxed paper. After washing her hands thoroughly and drying them well, she reached into the flour bag and put a handful in the middle of the waxed paper. She shook out an even amount of cornmeal from the box onto the flour, mixing the two together with her fingers. Going to the stove, she poured some olive oil into the skillet, covering the bottom of the pan about a quarter inch deep, and turned on the pilot light. When the flame did not light, she turned it off again and found a wooden match in a little black cast iron metal holder shaped like a log cabin that hung next to the stove. After smelling around the burner to be sure the propane had dissipated, she struck the match, holding the flame close to the burner again as she turned the round white stove handle. The pilot flame jumped to life.

Leaving the burner on high, Lea went back to her fish, salted them inside and out and rolled them in the flour and cornmeal mixture, sprinkling a little inside the slit in each belly. The oil in the pan was beginning to smoke. She turned the fire down to medium. Lifting each fish by its head one at a time, she gently shook off the excess flour and cornmeal mixture then laid them side by side into the skillet, careful not to splash her hand with the hot oil. Soon the entire cabin was filled with the smell of cooking trout.

All the time that Lea worked, Karl leaned against the kitchen wall, watching every move she made. For all the attention she paid him, he could have been invisible.

If the plates and cups of the cabin were matched at all, it would be the dents and scratches of a hundred years' worth of use. They were made of memories, and Lea secretly thought them priceless. Making no effort to set the table in a womanly manner, old bent forks were tossed on the table. There was no need to wash the time-worn wood. It was scrubbed clean.

Lea rummaged around in a cupboard, finding a can of cut green beans she opened with an ancient can opener found in the utensil drawer. If she were ever in danger of losing a finger, it was then. Still, she got no help from the invisible Karl. She poured the beans into a small pot, added vinegar, pepper, and a huge stirring spoon. The beans would be served cold.

The burner was turned off. Each fish fried to a crispy brown on both sides was taken from the skillet with a spatula, then slid upon a chopping board she had covered with paper towels to absorb the oil. The board was placed on the table along with the salt shaker, a bottle of apple juice, and new loaf of wheat bread that was found in the old refrigerator. Lea mentally checked off her food group: *meat, vegetable, grain, fruit. No milk? Next time. It was time to eat.*

Lea sat down at the table, bowed her head in silent prayer, and dove into the meal as if she had not eaten in a week. Soon the invisible Karl grabbed a plate, plopped the two remaining fish upon it, spooned out all the green beans except for two left floating in the vinegar and pepper fluid, and poured himself a cup of juice. He reached into the bag of bread and took out nearly half in one handful. With a slap of the screen door, he was gone.

Darkness had settled over the lake valley before Karl came back through the cabin door. The air had cooled as the sun dipped below the mountain range, and so Lea had closed the outer door. Karl found his way to the sink with his dishes he had rinsed in the creek that ran beside the cabin and into the lake.

Moonlight glowed through the kitchen window, and he could see that the room had been cleaned and neatened. The homey scent of their dinner warmed the air mixing with the clean smell of lavender lingering there. He had always favored it, the lavender scent left on Lea's skin and clothing he presumed was left there from her bath soap, for it was almost non-detectable. Being a field soldier made it at times impossible to bathe properly, though marines were taught ways to get by on as little water as possible, which was not always an asset as his days in the field were many for him and his squad. Body odor was something he never grew used to, especially his own. But somehow that very keen sense of smell now made those months worthwhile. The scent of lavender had become precious to him.

Karl knew that Lea chose to sleep on the couch by the window. Her two travel bags were in the corner beside the smoke-stained, river-rock fireplace. There was a steep narrow stairway to an upper loft of the *A*

Frame cabin with the most comfortable king-sized bed he had ever slept on. A tall window looked out over the lake. One wall was opened with a lodge-pole railing built-in to keep one from carelessly ending up off the edge and down onto the living room rug.

The cabin was small with a very small bathroom. The shower barely fit him or his dad. In summer months, they preferred to soak in the creek where a pool formed in one sandy place. It was a perfect area for kids to play as the grown-ups sat in lawn chairs and relaxed on the small sandy beach while the warm sun filtered through the quaking aspen tree leaves of summer. The small beach was used more than the lake area when family came to visit.

Close by, a level clearing was used for extra sleeping quarters. If Lea stayed, he would put up a tent and move outdoors to give her the cabin. It pleased him to think of her being here. In fact, it pleased him too much. He had actually been mourning their separation when that lavender scent of hers hit him like a ton of bricks. He went down to the lake to fish but found he did not have the heart for it. The events of the day before kept going around in his head. If he had time to learn more about Philip from Jacob, perhaps he may have been able to deal with the old man's misgivings.

Philip was so distrusting of his relationship with his granddaughter, Karl knew there was a serious reason behind it. It had to be something from their past. But he knew the importance of not prying into such a delicate matter. His medical ethics were so deeply ingrained he could not and would not step over any line to intrude into such a private situation. Simply speaking, it was none of his business.

So when Philip asked him in no uncertain terms to pack his bags and "come with him," he did exactly as told. He believed that his non-interference could impress the old man as no argument ever could in his own self-defense. There was an envelope placed in his hand containing a stack of one hundred dollar bills before both he and Jacob left him in the hotel lobby. Karl knew better then to refuse the money. He had suspected what was in the envelope, but out of respect he shook his hand, Jacob's hand, and watched the two men leave the building knowing that the old man's love for his granddaughter must be awesome for him to treat his guest in such a manner, being the gentleman he was.

Karl knew that he had to call Lea, but he wanted to make it as painless as possible. He wanted her to know that his being there was okay. There were friends in Denver he planned to call keeping him from actually lying to her. But he thought, with some guilt, there was always a chance to change his mind and fly out on the next plane to Nevada where he would eventually end up at his dad's cabin beside the lake.

He had always felt at home in the secluded area. Any neighbors were several miles away. It was the hideaway he longed for, and it was time to think away from Lea Renton. Shc had a way of distracting him as no woman had ever done. The very thought had him worried. Just as he was beginning to put some distance between them, she showed up literally on his doorstep. Well, when one was not sure how to proceed; the best thing to do was to burrow down and watch one's adversary. That's what he planned to do. But first, he would do his best to send her back lickety-split to her grandfather. Things could not be right in that corner of her world. If that didn't work, there was the tent area for his camp. He would set it up in the morning for his own quarters. *No way would he sleep anywhere near that lavender scent of hers!*

Karl took the stairs to the loft two steps at a time as usual. They were so creaky under his weight he sometimes wondered if one day he might fall through them. There was no need to change the bed sheets. He never used the ones supplied. His sleeping bag was laid out upon the bed, so after quickly rolling it up and packing up his clothing, he headed downstairs to gather up some toilet articles from the miniature bathroom. Reaching inside the linen closet in the hallway, he pulled out a set of neatly folded sheets and headed toward the sofa where Lea lay fully dressed on her back with an arm resting over her eyes.

"Yes?" she asked without moving.

"Your upstairs room is ready except for these." After tossing the folded sheets onto her stomach with a plop, he slammed out the door.

11

One morning after breakfast, Lea found a restless Karl scowling down at her from where he leaned against the kitchen sink. Looking up at him from where she sat reading, she asked, "So, is the shower too small for you? Can you stand to bathe in the stream in the winter months?"

Karl blinked. "I can bathe in the shower. I'm not that big."

"I would apologize about hurting your feelings about the 'shower being too small' remark, but you are rather large in an, um—attractive kind of way."

Karl looked at her suspiciously where she sat with her Bible opened before her. She looked like an angel, but he knew better and ignored the "attractive" comment altogether.

"I bathe. Just where I do is none of your concern. He took a sip of the coffee that he had to admit was quite good. It was still dark outside. She was early to rise and that coffee scent seemed to reach him every morning even in the sleeping quarters he had set up downstream.

The old light bulb that hung from its simple thick electrical cord over the table cast a glow about her where she had been focusing on her study. She wore reading glasses that only complimented her looks. When she looked up, slipping them off to focus on him, he knew he was in for her sass. *No. She was no angel.*

"It's not such a small shower as you seem to think," Lea said.

"I never said it was small. You did. I don't use it anyway in warm weather because the—"

"Yes? The creek pool works better because?"

"How would you know where I bathe?" Karl growled.

"I'm not blind, you know. I only wear these glasses to read with to keep my eyes from any kind of strain. Therefore, I have the eyes of—why, the eyes of an eagle!"

Seeing that he wore his famous "frown face," she hid a smile.

"Well," she said casually, "can you blame a girl? That view from the loft window is wonderful and—well—I'll just come right out and say it. We women sometimes do need an incentive to get up in the morning. *My* goodness! I knew a young man once who practiced that face in the mirror for Halloween night. Be sure not to use it around small children, will you?"

With that, she rinsed her cup, set it on the edge of the window sill, and trotted upstairs to dress for her morning run.

The summer days seemed to slow time after the rushed hours of military duty. Karl knew to treasure them, especially the time spent with Lea. Some days she seemed laid back, other days she seemed restless.

Today appeared to be one of her more restless moods. Though outwardly calm in appearance, he could sense a watchfulness in her. *Was it a discomfort in being close to him?* She had given him his music lesson for the day as usual, and outwardly she acted no differently, but he was learning to know her more intimately as time passed.

Tonight, Lea's bedroom light from the cabin woke Karl as it peaked through the pine boughs that shielded her upstairs view from his sleeping area. He glanced at the fluorescent dial on his wrist watch. She had barely turned out the lights in her room for the night, and was up again. For whatever reason she could not sleep, she would find comfort in her music. The guitar she kept with her wherever she traveled and her music sheets that were filled with her latest creations were her only companions. Lea was truly an artist with words, and it was all about people, places, everyday life. Some of her songs were about the wonder of living in the beauty of her world, and all of the words were woven with such intricacy; nevertheless, with a kind of simplicity…

Though it was an obvious invasion of her privacy, Karl once again found himself moving towards the cabin porch to listen to the soft sound of her voice, the gentle sound as her fingers moved over the strings of her guitar. If it were possible to make love with music, it was Lea. And the lyrics she sang flowed like a warm summer breeze filling his soul, seeping into his bones like the warmth of sunlight after a cold winter's night.

Karl had left his laptop computer behind to force himself the separation from human contact, for he needed to clear his mind for a time from all distractions. But now he felt an intense longing to find out more about the business affairs of this woman who was determined not to let anything interfere with the promise of her three month's time with him. As he remembered back to the gossip from the musicians' leisure time in Las Vegas about her songwriting talents and the success of her work with other musicians in the music industry, he needed to know more.

Lea used a name to disassociate her with her success. Why? He guessed that the fame that came with the talent she possessed simply was not important to her. She seemed to want the privacy to create her masterpieces that were literally life-changing if one listened to the message there—if one could get past the dreamy sound of her voice.

Now as he sat in the quiet night where he could hear the words of her newest work, even the crickets seemed to interrupt their courtship chirping, content to listen. It was coming together with ease as did the previous two she had completed since coming to the cabin.

First she completed the lyrics with the gentle strumming of her guitar. Over and over she repeated the verses until they were perfected, as was her way. When she set the guitar carefully aside, he knew that her light would be on until the early morning hours. Wasting no time, sheets of paper would be filled with her precise print. And arranged above and below the letters were the symbols that she knew so well and yet looked so strange to him. The sheets were then signed, scanned, and e-mailed to her secretary, Jerry Handly, whom she trusted them with from that time on. Only when Handly needed her original signature would he request a face-to-face meeting with her, which had been set up some weeks in advance.

Sometime in the night, Karl had dozed in the comfortable old rocker that his dad favored on his visits to the cabin. When he awakened, the morning sun rising from the east behind the cabin was lighting the tree line at the mountain range before him. He could smell Lea's fresh brewed coffee and faintly hear the sound of the pot percolating on the burner. From long ago, he could remember that old dented tin pot with the tiny glass bubble that fit on its lid where the water would shoot up into it, turning a darker and darker brown until the rich smell of coffee filled every inch of the cabin. Some modern changes in the design of the new drip coffee machines were definitely not for the better! Yes, that sound and smell coming from that old-time invention bumping on the burner went back to his earliest memories at the cabin. Fun days with his dad, and old dogs, and fishing, and hiking, and the good old boys that would visit, so filled up with old time humor and stories to fill a kid's mind with dreams of tomorrows when the real dreams were being fulfilled at that very moment. It caused an ache in his chest to know that those days were past, and he had had so few of them. And now Lea would add to his memories of his days spent in this place, and he longed to stop time.

From this day forward, whenever he sat on the old porch listening to that old pot bumping on the burner and smelling its magic scent, she would fill his thoughts until his brain could no longer function. *Yes. She had become a part of the rhythm of his existence, and he had only known her for such a short time.* Karl frowned into the beautiful morning of the mountain basin. Lifting himself from the rocker, he murmured a grumpy, "Good going, Dad!"

12

"So, let us focus. We've outlined the history of music from the days of the beginning of man." Lea grinned to herself as she watched Karl grit his teeth. Treating him like a school boy was one of the pleasures of her day. "You've learned the basic music score, symbols, differences in—let us check off all of your accomplishments in our minds. You are such a fast learner! Okay, okay, okay. You've done so well in such a short time! Be proud. Now, let me ask *you* for a change. What more do you want to learn about music?"

Karl set down the backpack he had been cramming with supplies. It contained a hatchet, extra knife, compass, flash light, small mirror, dry food, coffee, small pot and skillet, salt, cooking oil, fishing line and hooks, first aid kit, space blanket, flint, wooden matches each wrapped separately and stored inside a waterproof pouch, one large trash bag, a long leather boot lace, and a pair of socks. His tightly rolled military sleeping bag was ready to strap on top of the pack once buckled closed. He wore military clothing from his hat down. The revolver strapped onto his hip made him look entirely the macho man, but Lea decided she had teased him enough.

The morning sun glared off the watch that seemed to be such a part of his wrist, flashing sunlight into Lea's eyes from its glass face as he worked on the outdoor log bench that was as old as the cabin itself. It sat before the small tent that Karl had erected the day after Lea's arrival when he had failed to send her packing back to her Grandfather's estate.

Lea shifted her position, but only enough to keep the sun at her back, a tactical advantage. She watched as Karl finished his precise but somewhat hurried packing, buckle the backpack securely closed, tie his sleeping bag snugly on top, hoisting the pack's weight upon his thick back, and grin at her. "I'm ahead in my studies, so I'm taking a few days off. You see, I've been taking night courses—*Music Appreciation*."

Karl watched her cheeks grow pink with embarrassment. Lea did not embarrass easily, and he knew that she had not suspected his attendance of her late-night work sessions. Some of her songs were ones she had never put to paper but sang only to her Holy Family. They were intimate and personal.

"So. One's privacy is a word that means little to Dr. Karl Benson."

"Practice what you preach, Little Missy."

"I've been invited inside your precious space, my good Doctor."

"Don't call me good. No one is good but our Heavenly Father." He turned to disappear into the forest.

Lea brightened. "Well said. Where are we going and how long will we be away?"

Karl froze in his tracks. "*I* will be away for three days. Mrs. Gadison who stays here when the family is away will be sharing the cabin with you, so you're not alone."

"There is some cleaning and stocking up on kitchen supplies to be done. I'll leave her a note." She turned to walk back toward the cabin.

"You'll not find me, so don't even try," he called back.

"See ya, Doc."

Stopping in midstride, he cocked his head to one side. *Had he actually growled? She was making him crazy! What if she got lost tracking him? Well, it would be fun watching her try.*

Karl watched from an vantage point where Lea would have no way of spotting him. She left the cabin thirty minutes later dressed in clothing left by the boys when they visited the cabin. Her outfit included camo hunting pants, matching shirt, hiking boots, leather gloves, and a comical bush hat that would wisely shade her face, neck, and ears from sunburn. Around her neck she had tied a blue bandana, probably found in Hank's dresser drawers. A backpack complete with attached sleeping bag was strapped onto her back, and the rifle she carried in her right hand completed her ensemble.

It's too heavy a load. Karl grinned. But to his surprise, she headed for the lake instead of trying to locate his tracks where she had last seen him.

As he followed at his distance, he watched her unloaded her things beside the boathouse, expertly flip over and load his favorite canoe with her gear, and enter the hut to emerge buckling on a life jacket. Pushing off into the lake and sliding in as slick as any Native American local, she began paddling along the shoreline humming as she glided along.

Karl had to smile. She thoroughly outsmarted him! It would be a feat of endurance to keep up with her by land. But to lose sight of her would make it almost impossible to find where she would come ashore. So Karl moved at a brisk pace knowing Lea paddled the canoe slowly enough that he could keep up. When the sweat began to dampen his clothing and he could feel the weight of his pack, he had to admire her strategy once again. She knew he would of course stay close, worrying over her safety in the wilderness area.

A community of houses would soon cut off the privacy of their adventure, so Lea decided it was time to beach and dock the canoe and unload her supplies. She managed to pull it a safe way upon the sand and hid the oar she used, and a matching one kept inside, in some thick brush some way from the boat in case it was discovered. She began to make her way into the forest marking her trail as she went by breaking small twigs along the way.

Finding a clearing a half mile into the forest where a spring flowed from a rock-face in the hillside, Lea thankfully set down her gear. She knew the ice cold water would be safe from any animal or other contamination that could be found upstream as it came out of the mountainside pure from the winter snow melt-off. Filling the canteen and cooking pot she had carried, she set them within the clearing, rolled out the sleeping bag, and laid the rifle cocked and ready beside her, falling immediately to sleep in the warmth of the sun that shown through the tall evergreen boughs of the forest.

When Lea awoke, Karl had a small campfire made and was boiling the pot of water she had collected earlier. Watching from where she lay, he took a handful of coffee from a bag in his pack and dumped it into the water. After a couple minutes, the pot was taken from the coals and set upon a rock close to the heat of the fire, waiting, she knew for the grounds to settle in the bottom.

Karl knelt on one knee, watching her as she watched him. Finally, she sat up to open the bolt on the rifle for safety and placed it again beside her on the bed. When Karl took her a tin cup of steaming coffee, she sipped it thankfully.

"I have another cup in my pack."

"This will do for now," Karl said, setting the pot on the ground next to him where he rested his back against a large, fallen log. The ground was not as clean as a sandy beach area because of the last year's fall foliage, but runoff rain and snow water kept it fairly so within the clearing area. "You don't sleep much."

"I usually don't need much." She found it strange to have slept so soundly with Karl moving around the camp.

"Tell me about yourself," he said.

Lea became instantly alert. Something had changed between them since she had come to the cabin. Finally, today, Karl was open to her counsel, and she was not sure as to how to proceed. He was not one to talk to as she would one of her youths about her faith in her Lord Jesus Christ. And Karl was already a Christian, faithful and true. But he had been tested, she sensed painfully so, and he needed a fellow Christian to help him find his way back to the counsel of the true comforter, the Holy Spirit.

Lea set her empty cup upon the sleeping bag, her head bent in thought. What Holy Spirit asked of her took her breath away. She had not given her testimony to this extent to a living soul. But the quiet words he spoke were unmistakable. To disobey was not an option.

When Lea looked up, Karl was watchful, waiting. She glanced around at their perfect camp spot. It was simple and perfect. The late afternoon sun peaked through the evergreens that blanketed the hillside. The crystal clear water trickling out of the rock face would be all the drink and wash water they needed for the night and next morning. In the stream were brook trout to feed them, and they both had carried coffee and dry food enough for nourishment. Clothing and sleeping bags would warm their bodies throughout the cool nighttime hours; hats and clothing would protect them from the sun come daylight again. They were both young and healthy of mind, successful individuals in their own right, living in one of the most beautiful and bountiful countries of the world. And both were blessed with people who loved and cared about them.

God's blessings rained down more than the sands of his earth's creation. "Thank you, my Lord!" Lea whispered into the clean mountain air.

Karl did not hear the words but wondered at them. Lea was so deep in thought he worried if he had asked too painful a question but could not retract his request. He absolutely had to know about her, who she was, of her beginning. She finally looked across at him. "Alright. My story. But first let us eat." She stood, went to him reaching out for the empty pot. The log where he leaned would be the best place for her to sit beside him to tell her story, but it would take time.

While Karl fished the stream for the small trout that dwelled there, Lea carried water and heated it on their small, contained camp fire. Having fed it carefully with dead logs and twigs to keep any sparks at a safe distance from the trees and bushes surrounding their campsite, they had built up a good bed of coals. The small skillet Lea had carried in her pack with oil, salt, flour, and cornmeal mixture for the fish was worth the weight. It was a luxury she would not have managed if not for the help of the lake travel.

After they ate their meal together, both were satisfied with the trout Karl had caught, cleaned, and cooked. Two small pots of herbal tea water now stayed warm by the fire. With a flashlight each for nighttime, Lea was wrapped in her sleeping bag and both were snuggled against the weathered log Karl had pulled close to their campfire for the night. They seemed like two young people ready to tell scary stories, except for the seriousness of their mood. Karl forced himself to relax in an effort to comfort her. As a doctor in psychiatry, he knew it was best not to help a patient along with a life story or experience. *But Lea was not a patient. She was what?*

She now smiled at him a little sadly. "Alright, Karl. To begin, I was born in New York City. My father was an architect and successful at his trade from a young age, therefore quite independent of my Grandfather Philip. Nonetheless, they were very close. My father met my mother at a company party when he was forty years old. She was thirty-two and already a renowned surgeon. Her family had come to the States from Ireland for a short time for her father's business interests. Mother decided to stay and attend a university here, earning her medical degrees, and soon considered herself an American, which did not go over well with her father. An older sister came for a visit one summer and also stayed to marry an American, which further alienated the daughters with their Irish father.

"When my parents decided to marry, it broke up both families. Grandfather Philip disowned my father, having had issues with my mother's independent, outspoken 'unladylike' nature and so on. And my other grandfather disowned my mother for—well—you get the picture.

"Father bought a home in downtown New York, but both of my parents preferred to spend as much time at a second home in the suburbs. This is where their children would experience an upbringing out of the city as much as possible. I was born three years after my parents were married. Both wanted a larger family, but my mother had a difficult time conceiving. I was a kind of 'miracle' baby, they called me.

"My childhood was like a dream. Mother gave up her career for me. My dad accepted jobs only in the New York area so we could be a family. Mother home schooled me. What she did not feel accomplished enough at instruction, tutors would be called in. But she was my classmate. We did everything together. The only person I was closer to was my father. I could not begin to explain to you how much I still miss him. I won't even try. Excuse me a moment."

The night air made Lea shiver when she got up to refill their cups from the pot balanced on a rock beside the fire. After snuggling back into her sleeping bag next to Karl where he sat, she met his eyes through the steam from her cup.

"When I was sixteen, on New Year's Eve night, friends were calling for us to make our annual New Year's Eve party in New York City. Our house staff was always given a full month off for the Christmas holiday, and I was alone at the country house. It was the first year I did not attend with mother and father. When the police officers came to inform me that there had been an accident, they did not guess my age." Lea shrugged, excusing the officers.

"After they left, I dressed in one of Mother's suits and drove the car into town. I'd been driving with father for some years on the narrow roads in case of an emergency situation. When I dressed up, there weren't many people I could not fool as to knowing my real age. It was a game we played." Lea gave Karl a slightly impish look that made his heart ache. Her next words would be unbelievable if he didn't know her so well.

"So, I drove to the city morgue. It was easy. I showed my fake I.D. I always carried with me and saw for myself it was true. They were mine."

Lea watched Karl's face turned pale in the firelight.

"It was then I knew that Holy Spirit was standing with me in that glaring room. As I stood beside those cold, steel tables, I could feel his warmth. That was when I learned to focus on the reality of my father's heavenly body, and my mother's heavenly body. Not to mourn the passing of their earthly ones. If our Lord's purpose was for them to be in a perfect sleep for a time, or to awaken instantly with him in consciousness was not my concern. My focus was to trust in him with all of my energy.

"So we walked out together, Holy Spirit and me. We went home, laid down beside our Christmas tree for the last time, and slept. The next morning Mother's sister, husband, and kids showed up bright and early to take over the funeral arrangements and everything else, including me. I called in our family lawyer and asked him to do what was necessary to make them leave, got together clothing to take to the mortuary, packed my bags, and closed up the house. Three days later was the service. I left instructions for the lawyer to sell both homes and furnishings. He is still my lawyer to this day. He was my father's choice, and he is mine. He did not let me down when I needed him.

"When Grandmother found me, I was on a road trip with my first band, singing in a bar in Houston, Texas. It wasn't the best place for us to meet, but she was great about it. Tough as they come. I was crazy about her from the first, but it took time for Grandfather and me to bond. We did not like one another at first. That is another story." Lea laughed. "Anyway, after a couple of months, he began to spoil me rotten. We still butt heads occasionally. You see, Grandfather thinks he's an atheist—"

Karl did not sleep. When the morning sun began to light the sky, he got up and walked out a ways from camp to wash up in the stream and think. In all his years he had heard some fantastic stories, but Lea's was to say in the least, remarkable. It would take some time to sort it out, if ever. People forever continued to surprise him, but she went way beyond that.

13

It was fish for breakfast. Karl had left for an upstream pool only moments before when Lea felt the signal of her pager she always kept inside her clothing, close to her heart. The plan was that if Grandfather was to ever become seriously ill, Jacob would signal her on her pager's special line. It had been necessary through the years to wear it for her peace of mind. Only when it was tested at a certain time once each month to know if it was working properly did Lea feel the slight hum of its presence.

This morning, she had freshened up and brushed her teeth at a secluded spot she'd found a short distance downstream. When she returned, Karl had already neatened up their camp area and was heading out to catch their breakfast.

So there would be no question as to the urgency of the signal, the pager beeped three times within a minute, but after the first one, Lea was already scratching out a note for Karl. She would secure it to his backpack explaining the emergency, and that she would leave the rifle locked inside the cabin's gun case where she borrowed it from. Leaving all else for time's sake, Lea had covered the distance back to the lake and was stowing the two short paddles into the canoe when strong hands took hold of her from behind spinning her around.

"Karl! You could have warned me!"

"What good is a rifle when you are oblivious to what is going on around you?" he growled. "If I were a bear or a mountain lion, you would be dead!"

"My mind was on other things. I've no time to argue the point. I'll leave word at the store when I find out how Grandfather is doing."

"No you won't because I'm going with you."

Lea closed her eyes while taking a deep breath. He had seen her do it countless times, a practice of hers when her patience was wearing thin. When she opened her eyes again, Karl was frowning down at her. His advantage in height was a full head taller, and he outweighed her significantly. And strength wise, she didn't stand a chance.

He was so close; Lea could smell the wood smoke from their campfire on his clothing. For no matter what reason, the fire would not be left unattended. He must have returned for something shortly after she left, and after reading her note, doused and stirred the coals until not one was a threat to the forest before setting out. So as a sprinter, even dodging trees, branches, and brush, he had made remarkable time catching up to her.

Lea bowed her head with eyes closed once again. *Holy Spirit. Please Lord, let your will be done.* She turned and climbed into the front end of the canoe feeling it dip low as Karl's weight slid in behind her. The remarkable craft sliced through the water as they glided out into the glassy calm of the lake, while the only sounds heard were the distant chirping of birdlife and the quiet dip of his oar into the water as it pushed them along. Lea picked up the second oar, and soon they had their rhythm as they moved along. The moment would have been perfect except for the fact that Grandfather's life could be ending at that very moment, or he could already be gone from them.

Lea was quiet. She was not surprised when Karl took over their journey to Sun Valley, Idaho. The actual drive time to the airport from the cabin would possibly parallel their flight time to the valley and Grandfather's estate. She was especially grateful when he took the clipboard from her hand and began the checklist of her small aircraft before takeoff.

Karl had wasted no time driving the narrow roads from the cabin to the airport but still took no chances with their lives or the lives of others. The only disadvantage to Lea in letting him take over the details of their travel was that it gave her more time to think of the possibilities going on at home. When they reached an area of clear cell phone coverage, she found out from a call to Jacob that Grandfather had a heart attack or stroke. He was at home being treated by his ancient hometown doctor with the latest medications, but his prognosis was grim. She had to prepare herself. If it was his time, she must be ready to let him go.

She and Grandfather had a pact. They had discussed it and were both comfortable with their agreement. She knew of his wishes, and he knew of hers if she were to die before him or become seriously ill. It was time to honor his requests.

It was strange sitting in the copilot seat, but Lea welcomed it. Karl was an excellent pilot, which was no surprise to her. But still it made her think about how little she knew of him. She only knew that he was a child living in a placement home run by child services when Hank found him at the age of twelve and brought him to his home in Texas. He was Hank's first adopted son. Hank now had two children that lived with their mother and chose to ignore him. Lea thought of their loss in not knowing their father. She would do her best not to judge; it just made her sorry for them for he was such a fine man to know. In fact, she had to be careful not to fall in love with him, no matter what their age difference.

When the plane's tires touched down onto the runway that Lea knew so well, she felt strangely calm. As they had circled in for a landing, her uncle's car was spotted in the driveway, along with two others that she was unfamiliar with. She now prepared herself for a confrontation. For years now, Lea knew to keep these times focused to avoid confusion. She would do what had to be done out of respect for her grandfather's wishes. Knowing the plan, as they rehearsed it together in his office throughout the years for his peace of mind, in no way was her uncle to be allowed to interfere with his instructions.

Jacob had sent Miguel, Juanita's husband, to meet them at the private airstrip immediately upon landing. He gave Lea the keys to the car and nervously explained in Spanish that two business men he had never seen before had met her uncle at the house two hours earlier.

Lea wondered who had informed her uncle or anyone else of Grandfather's medical condition. Jacob was faithful knowing that the doctor alone was to be informed of any emergency and then Lea.

When she stepped through the wide front door, there were three darkly suited men facing her from the office doorway. Karl's presence was gratefully felt directly behind her. When their eyes shifted upward to him, Lea felt immediate satisfaction.

"Jacob?" she called out, her eyes never leaving her uncle's face.

"Yes, Ms. Lea!" he called down from the top of the stairway.

"Do you have your can of mace in hand for intruders?"

"Yes!"

"And these gentlemen know that you are prepared to use it if they should come anywhere near Grandfather's door?"

"They know they will, hopefully, be only temporarily blinded by it and will need to seek medical attention if they reach the top of the staircase."

"Thank you, Jacob."

"These immature tactics of yours, child, will get you nowhere. The sheriff is on his way along with medical personnel to transport your grandfather to a proper medical facility."

Lea pulled her cell phone from her belt and without looking at it clicked in a number with one hand. "Sheriff McKinney? Lea Renton. What is your location? Very good. Thank you." She clicked the phone off, hooking it back in place on her belt. "I suggest that you three leave these premises immediately. Legally, Uncle, I have a restraining order registered against you at the county office. If you do not comply with my request, you may find yourself having your next meal in the city jail."

Lea did not wait to watch her uncle's face turn red with rage. She simply turned and trotted up the stairs to attend to her grandfather's needs. When the men looked at Karl, he shrugged his shoulders and took a seat by the front door.

14

Grandfather's bedroom was more like an elegant hotel suite. Lea avoided looking toward his empty chair placed so close beside Grandmother's where she had sat with him such a short time ago. All the memories were there—the feel of her head resting upon his chest, the strong beat of his heart, the starched feel of his white dress shirt against her cheek, and lastly, the clean smell of him that was his own.

The remembered glare of that sterile room where her parent's bodies lay so many years ago spread like an opened tomb before her. Lea knew that she was vulnerable to doubt, and she would not let Satan have his way. Her walk with Holy Spirit was too precious a comfort. She would choose *his* counsel, always. She thought with firm purpose: *The morgue is simply a facility to assure proper respect of the human body. The people who work there are a blessing to the living and a blessed respect to the bodies of loved ones passed. It is not a place to be feared. I will not let it become so. Old fantasies encouraging evil thoughts will not distract me from my Lord's purpose!* Lea could feel her confidence in her Savior return Satan to a safe distance where he belonged, so she could now move forward.

"Ms. Lea. Is that you?"

"Dr. Ethan? Yes, I am here."

The doctor came into the sitting room from the bedroom and motioned for Lea to be seated on the sofa. He chose to sit beside her, taking her hand in his.

"Jacob called me about seven o'clock this morning. Your grandfather had not shown up for breakfast, and there was no response when he tried to awaken him. When I examined him an hour later, Philip was still unresponsive, so I began the IV—a blood thinner and simple hydrator. So far there has been no change."

She nodded. "In your experience, have any patients of this nature regained consciousness?"

He patted her hand. "Almost none. And if this is a stroke of the magnitude I believe it to be, his chances are not good. Of course with no testing, because of his documented request, there is no way to tell how extensive the damage. The good news is that there are no signs of discomfort, and I believe that he is not aware of his surroundings. It is as if he has already left us. And now if you will allow me to elaborate? Being an old man myself, if I were to choose an end to this life, this 'kind of sleep' would be in no way objectionable. Still, I have seen amazing things in my days. There is always a chance that he could regain consciousness."

"What does he need, Dr. Ethan?"

Lea watched the old gentleman carefully stand as elderly men do. She was very fond of him. He was highly intelligent, continually studying the newest medical discoveries, and she fully trusted him. Knowing that he had heard her question, she followed him as he gathered his medical bag that sat on the small table beside the bedroom door.

"You tell me." He turned to her. "I see you're already thinking it out with those excellent brain cells of yours."

Alright. Two male nurses for her modest and distinguished grandfather would be hired immediately. And she would stay close, so a sleep chair would be ordered and delivered right away.

"I will hire two male nurses. They will be at your office to be interviewed. If you have any doubts as to their competence, you will let me know?"

"Understood. The IV is set until nine, and the bag will then need changing. Jacob has been instructed as to its use. It is simple, but you may help him if necessary. He is a bit rattled, although he has done quite well. I will return tomorrow. This you must know. It would not be kind to continue the IV if your grandfather's body is trying to shut down. I will continue it for three days and then discontinue the treatment. Keeping him comfortable is the most important thing you can focus on right now. Read to him. Talk to him. You will know what to say. There is some belief that a comatose patient may find comfort in the sound of a loved one's voice."

Lea took his hand into both of hers. "You've not failed us, Dr. Ethan. Thank you."

The old man looked into her eyes. "You take so much onto your shoulders, child. Remember, you are human like the rest of us."

"I will remember," she assured the doctor, who was much more a friend.

It took thirteen days for Philip Renton to die. Lea only left his side to let the nurses bathe him under Jacob's watchful eye, take a daily walk while Jacob sat vigil, or attend to her own personal needs. The trays of food that Juanita encouraged Lea to eat were barely touched. Her main nourishment was broth and her favorite herbal tea. Karl thought that she would seek comfort in her music but was surprised that she did not.

The stamina of the human body never failed to amaze Karl. Philip had not eaten or taken any fluids since his third day on IV and continued to draw breath day after day.

As the two male nurses took immaculate care of him, Karl knew that any other medical assistance was avoided per his own request. The old doctor visited once daily assuring them there was no pain. Jacob questioned him often on Lea's welfare, but his only advise was to "leave her be." Karl knew that she would stay by her grandfather's side, protecting him from any outside interference as was her promise to him, until he either awakened or drifted off into his rest.

Lea read to him daily or played books on CD, something her grandfather had always enjoyed. His care was all legal, all was preplanned, all were his own wishes. Karl could see no fault in it, only admiration in Lea's faithfulness to her grandfather. On the thirteenth day, Lea calmly came downstairs, nodded at Karl who was watching Jacob tend his roses, and took the old man by the hand leading him into the garden to inform him of his friend's death.

The service was within three day's time. He was buried beside his wife. Lea was allowed by Philip to design her grandmother's headstone and it was understood when the time came she would design his. Karl had visited the gravesite one day while on a drive with Jacob. The first marker with its dates included read, *His Beloved Lady*. He would guess that Philip Renton's would read, *Her Beloved Gentleman…*

"Child! This will always be *your* home!"

Lea's bags were packed and sitting outside the front door. "Wherever you are, Jacob, will always be my home. But now it is legally in your name. It was Grandfather's wish, and it is mine. And as you know, the cottage and its two acres are in Miguel's and Juanita's names. You are a family, as you have always been. Their children are your grandchildren, just as I have been your granddaughter and will always be."

Jacob smiled. "Thank you, Lea Ann. Now, where are you going?"

"I'm flying Karl home to his Texas ranch. Then—well—I've not decided. I will keep in contact." She kissed his cheek.

Lea reached down to gather her bags, but Karl was already putting them into the car. Miguel was driving them the short way to the plane. Her goodbyes were already said to his family.

As Lea turned to leave, Karl took the old man's hand in his. "Jacob. Stay busy."

"Son," Jacob said simply, passed the tears in his eyes.

15

Hank's home was as Lea had expected—the cowboy ranch of any kid's dreams. He had three boys now living at home. Samuel, the youngest of the three, was the only one present. The older boys were out of town on a Boy Scout trip for the month.

"Hey, kiddo," Hank greeted Lea with his gentle handshake. "How are you?"

"Getting by." She paused momentarily just to look at him. It was a joy just being close. He was energy giving, lifting her up, making life's burdens drift off into a distance while being with him.

"You'll stay awhile?"

"Perhaps an hour or so."

Karl simply raised his brows.

Hank nodded. His son was taking care of her, or trying his best to. That was more than pleasing to him. "Let's get you out of this Texas heat."

His boots made a clomping sound across the wooden porch. As he opened the creaky screen door, Lea thought back to the cabin she and Karl had spent so many hours at, and a surprising loneliness filled her. She would miss her time with him.

Hank's home was like walking back in history. Samuel and his brothers, or any boy for that matter, would be comfortable within its walls. She had visited the estate of the William S. Hart once and the place reminded her of it, except for the space. Hank's home was spacious, and she knew it had to be to house his adopted family.

Thump, the old family hound that had greeted them on the front porch, followed them in just far enough to collapse at the foot of a large man-sized easy chair where Lea guessed Karl would prefer to relax. It had a tall floor lamp beside it and a scarred wooden table. One could set a cup of hot coffee there without worry over causing any damage. The huge front window showed a lovely view of blue sky, alfalfa fields, and space as far as the eye could see, while a large side window looked out upon split rail corrals and old time barns free of any paint or varnish giving one a sense of gazing off into years past. No pipe corrals or metal buildings to detract from Hank's Western paradise. It was all Hank Benson, except for the modern conveniences and of course his nearby runway and hanger to house his necessary plane.

Lea sank down into Hank's worn cowhide sofa. There was a cup of iced tea placed into her hand by Karol, an elderly housekeeper, when Thump moved to rest his head upon her knee, inviting her to scratch behind a very long, thin ear. Samuel climbed up beside her to listen to the best of his Dad's "whopper" stories, when twenty minutes later Karl could see that Lea's eyes were getting heavy where the warm sun shone in upon her back through the window. He was relaxing in the oversized chair that Lea guessed was his own, and Hank had paused in his storytelling to sip at his mug of coffee, comfortably kicked back in a creaky rocking chair much like the one on the porch at the Lake Tahoe cabin.

"So, Ms. Lea! How fast can she go?"

Lea turned to look into the freckled face of Samuel only inches from her own and blinked. Karl had never seen her with a child of his age before and watched with interest as to how she would respond to him.

"Who might that be, Samuel?" she asked with all seriousness.

"My friends call me Sam, Ms. Lea. You can call me Sam."

"Thank you. My friends call me Lee. You may call me Lee, if you wish."

"Yep."

"So, Sam. How fast can who go?"

"Your plane, Lee. I'm guessing, well, maybe two hundred?"

"Well—"

The conversation between the two became quite focused on the aeronautics of the aircraft. Lea kept the discussion within the boy's ability to understand, not once talking down to the child. And all she told him was a lesson that he would learn from while Karl in turn, had learned something about her that was surprisingly pleasing to him.

Hank watched the scene unfold with interest. For the first time in his life, he knew his son to be totally focused on a woman. But a part of him became afraid that he had interfered too much. *Lord Jesus! I pray that this beautiful lady will not break his heart!*

"So. Can you take me up in her?" Samuel's round, green eyes were far too endearing.

Lea looked beseechingly to Hank who was no help whatsoever. He simply grinned at her dilemma.

That smile of hers! Karl's heart skipped a beat.

"We had better ask your Dad what he thinks," she said.

"Okay if we take her up for a spin, Dad?"

"You bet. If the lady promises to stay a night to rest up with us. Or forever."

Lea simply shook her head in surrender.

The next day, Hank invited Lea for an early morning ride to see some of the ranchland. She dressed in some borrowed clothes and found him in one of his barns saddling his favorite horse for her. Watching him move easily, as cowboys seem to do to conserve energy to get them through the long work days, she thought of how Hank was cowboy from the worn Stetson hat he favored to his scuffed leather boots. She had studied the Western wear of the cowboy and knew that every part of it had a purpose. The hat, neck scarf, long-sleeved shirt with snaps, tough denim jeans, thick rawhide chaps (that Hank would have no use for today), and high top boots with heals made to dig into the ground if need be. Many cowboys chose not to wear spurs or used them with a careful touch. Hank's walk, of course, today included the old time sound of spurs jingling with each step he took. And she suspected that if one were to look close enough, he would have a legitimate bow to his long legs from spending many years in the saddle.

"What do you know about horses, Lea Ann?" Hank asked as she watched him tighten the saddle's cinch strap around the sorrel's large barrel chest.

"I've learned how to tend to their needs. My basic riding style is English."

"How far did you go with it?"

"Dressage, some jumping competitions."

"So I was right. You're a Thoroughbred-type lady."

She laughed quietly. Her morning would in no way be boring.

Hank knew that Lea never talked much about herself, especially her own accomplishments. But he guessed that she was quite comfortable in the saddle, Western style, English, or bareback.

Texas was every bit as open as Lea had imagined it to be; and though it was the fall season, some days turned quite warm and so the early morning hour kept the air at a comfortable level. Lea, as usual, was sensible to protect her skin from the intense rays of the sun, nevertheless, she also enjoyed the feel of its warmth through her clothing and the clean smell of the dry outdoor air.

"You spend much time out of doors?" Hank asked after they had relaxed together for some time, listening to the clopping sound of their horses' hooves.

"Some. I traveled on a photo shoot of the central plains for two months with a friend last summer. He's a freelance photographer and writer. A few months later, we traveled the Amazon, but I left him to it after two weeks to catch up on my own work."

A rabbit jumped out of a clump of brush beside the trail, spooking both horses slightly. Neither Hank or Lea thought much about it.

"And you. Have you traveled?" she asked.

"In my younger years. The States, right here at home, have much to offer—and I traveled Europe, for a time. Austria is an awesome country, and I'm fond of her people. Now days? I'm content to travel in my rocking chair."

"And where do you visit, Mr. Benson?"

Hank gave her a crooked smile. "If I started telling you of my adventures, we'd be late for dinner, and you know it."

"Yes. I know it, but that is part of your charm."

"Is that what you call it? I thought it was the ramblings of a sixty-five-year-old entertainer."

"I think not. You have much to teach people. Have you thought about recording your adventures?"

"That's something to think about. But could anyone make heads-or-tails of it if one were to write them down?"

"I'm sure I could. Want to give it a try?" she asked.

"Now I do feel important," Hank said with a wink. "You know, little lady, I am truly indebted to you for spending these three months with Karl. How does he seem to cope with everyday routine?"

"You will never be in my debt, Henry Benson. Just knowing you is a privilege. As for your boy, yes, I have noticed signs of stress. And I have prayed for an answer just as you have. We must, of course, continue our prayer vigil.

"Now, in these three months our Lord has taught me some important things about Karl. He is a problem solver, he is very successful in his profession, and he is not accustomed to failure. But Karl has lived the reality of war, and for the second time in his life, he has found a hurt he cannot fix. Your son simply needs time to forgive himself for being human. He must hand this one over to the Lord."

Hank thought for several moments. "And the first hurt he could not fix?"

Lea gazed off into the vastness that was Texas. "That, I do not know."

16

One night turned into a week. It was as if Lea had come home, and it worried her how comfortably she fit in, how much she enjoyed watching Hank with Samuel. She quietly studied the way he worked with him and thought him remarkable. After dinnertime one cool and calm evening as they sat on the porch, the little boy started his usual questioning.

"Dad. It's so hard to be good. How can I remember everything so I can be in heaven with my mom when I get old like you someday?"

Lea turned away to hide a smile from where she sat on a front porch step, old Thump's head resting on her knee.

"Well, Sam, you could study your Bible all your life, and each time you did you would find more and more to study and learn about. That is good. But our Heavenly Father made it easy enough that everyone would know how to not only get into heaven but have the happiest life. Now, there are two rules that make all the difference. The most important rule to remember is to love our Lord Jesus Christ more than anyone or anything in our lives. The second rule is to care about each other. If we do those two things, we will be good and happy people now and someday in heaven."

"Would you write it down for me so I won't forget?"

"Well, Sam, that's the miracle of God's ways. You see, if I wrote it down, you might lose the paper. That's why God has now written it into your brain so you can never lose it."

"Yea, Dad. I won't lose it. It's stuck in there already."

"That's good, son. Now you get started to bed and we'll read some of our book tonight. And don't forget, I'm having a look at those choppers, so you better use some toothpaste this time."

"Okay. Night, Lee, night, Thump, night, Karl, night, Snoop. Night, everybody."

"Goodnight, Sam," they said as he crashed through the screen door, then reappeared to bestow upon Lea a giant hug around her neck and sloppy kiss upon her cheek. Whirling around, he shot back through the door once again.

Lea stood to walk away into the moonlit night, the lanky hound at her side. She hurt as she tucked away the precious feel of the little arms hugging her so tightly about her neck, the wet little kiss that still felt damp upon her cheek. Knowing how much she would soon be missing not only Samuel but this family that she had become so fond of, for the child's sake, it would be best to pack up and be on her way. Lea thought then of leaving Karl and the ache became almost unbearable, but leave him she must. There was so much of the Lord's work to be done, and he deserved a family life—something she could not give him. So many needed her. So many…

Hearing footsteps behind her, Lea knew without turning that they were Karl's. Somehow she felt a connection with him, which was strange having never experienced it with any man before. Of course there was Glen. The first man she thought was her soul mate for life. By ignoring the words of Holy Spirit, she pursued the union that had turned into a disaster. The man had lied most skillfully. He was handsome and crafty. She had put her trust in him first before all else in her life, and of course, that was her error. The secret to a life of peace, success, and safety is to love first her Lord Jesus with all her mind and heart and soul. Next comes the man in her life if he is meant to be, and *then* her children if she is so blessed. Many a devout Christian would argue the order putting their children first in their lives, but in error. By following Heavenly Father's plan, their children would have the parent's ultimate love and protection if placed third in their order of priorities. Heavenly Father's plan could be the only faultless one. And that was where she, Lea Ann Renton, had made the biggest mistake of her Christian life. She had put a man first in the order.

Glen Montgomery had fooled her completely, even joining with her in a false marriage and honeymoon that she thought would prove the happiest time of her life. Only upon arriving home after a month-long European tour with him did she learn from her grandfather that he was a fraud with a wife and children hidden away in Venice, Italy. Refusing to believe her grandfather, she had traveled a lonely journey to Italy to find him visiting a zoo with his beautiful wife and three young children. He had not seen her, and when she confronted him upon his arrival back in the States, he was totally surprised to find that her grandfather had him investigated and found him out.

Only by her quick wit did she stop her grandfather from harming the man; nevertheless, she was sure he would never show his face in the United States again. Even upon his death, Philip Renton would be a man of Glen Montgomery's most terrible nightmares if he should return, for her grandfather had friends that would be loyal for a lifetime, and the man knew better than to cross him.

Lea had later been able to pray for the man and for her grandfather—his intentions against him. It was all she could do. She then gave her mess over to the Lord to clean up for her as only he was able.

Now she had another man in her life, only this man was truly a good one. She would care for him by walking away, and would not involve him any longer in her life other than that of a Christian brother, for she must continue on with her ministry.

Lea went to a favorite place she had found to sit and pray. There was a bench that was built upon a rise overlooking the vast landscape of the ranch. The moon and starlit night was a dream to behold. Karl sat beside her, sharing the wonder of the moment. It was good, the way they could be together and say nothing at all. Just…be.

Minutes went by when Lea turned to face him and study his profile in the soft twilight.

"Yes?" he said.

"Your turn. Tell me about yourself."

Karl thought back to their time at the Tahoe Lake camp. The afternoon he had used those very words, and she had trusted him with her personal testimony. He knew there was more but what she told him said so much about who she was. It was not easy, the story about her mother and father's death. She had trusted him.

"The beginning?"

Lea thought for a moment. "It's a start."

"My first clear memory of my mother was when she left me at a shack in a dark end of town with a drunk by the name of Del. He was kind enough when he was drinking. He was not my father. There were many who could have been.

"She had hard eyes, my mother. He called her Angel. Her breath was sweet, her hair very light in color and long. She was tall and willowy and her voice was soft—gentle. She hit harder than he did.

"When I was old enough, she sold me to a group of men for some drugs. I was probably seven years old. Who knows? There was a crawl space beneath the shack that I managed to slip into and hide for the night. The next morning I tried to dig my way out but the ground was frozen, and I had only a broken board. If I made any noise they would have found me, so it was slow going. Late the next day, I made it out.

"I was a ways into the clean side of town when a young father let me into his house. He wouldn't let me anywhere near his kids, I stunk so badly. He had his wife fill a wash tub with hot water in the laundry room and scrubbed me as best he could. The man gave me some of his youngest son's cloths to wear. They were clean and soft and fine. I hated them. I felt like a beggar. When I asked for my clothes back, he said he burned them. It was the first time in my life I could remember wanting to cry.

"Right away a man and a woman from the home for unwanted kids came for me. The man never said goodbye…"

Karl was quiet for several moments. When he continued, his voice was void of emotion.

"The home I was taken to was a good one. I had friends there even if I wasn't a friend to them. They could have been my brothers, but I wouldn't let them. They liked me, and I never knew why. I could have helped them, they looked up to me, but I shut them out. I can still see their faces, especially the young ones. Yea, I did the necessary things if they needed something material, but there was one that wanted me to be like family to him, and I turned my back on him. He was sickly. I knew he wouldn't live long."

Knowing him, Lea said nothing. Finally, standing, she simply passed her hand over his head as she walked by, leaving him alone in the warm Texas night.

17

Summer had passed. Karl could see the signs. Lea was ready to move on and had already said her goodbyes to everyone but him. She was saving him for the last.

It was a sad morning for young Samuel. His Dad asked to "hitch a ride" as far as San Diego, California when he had learned of her destination plans. She was on her way to join up with a fellow musician. It was all the explanation given, all she needed to disconnect from her association with him. He was checked off her "to-do list."

They were now alone in the kitchen at daybreak, their usual coffee hour together, and he was quiet to the point of rudeness.

"I've left you some cleaning up to do at the lake." She set a cup of black coffee before him on the table.

"No problem."

"I'll send someone for my things. I owe you a sleeping bag. By now it has had some renters living in it where I left it up on the mountain, to be sure."

"Yea. Mine too. I'll go back to clean up and replace them both."

Lea leaned against the sink, sipping the steaming coffee from her cup, somewhere deep in thought. Then as if disappointed, she said, "I'd best get going. Your dad came for his coffee a while ago."

Karl shot up out of the chair nearly sending it over backward. "Just hold on. What was that all about?"

Lea made a face. "Just what was what all about?"

Karl scowled at her. There were just two steps between them, and if he took only one he could shake her until her teeth rattled.

"That look you just gave me. Like I was some kid that flunked a test you'd had high hopes for."

"Wow. You are at your old tricks, Dr. Benson. Reading my mind." She wondered if for once she had gone too far with him.

Karl was not amused. He was waiting for an explanation, and she was going nowhere until he got one.

After taking a long, deep breath, Lea turned away from him to meticulously wash, rinse, and dry her coffee cup as she spoke. "Alright. I always wanted a big brother. You were almost that brother."

Lea could feel him move behind her. Whenever he stood close, she could feel his presence, though they had seldom even touched. It was a kind of warmth whenever he so much as entered a room. No man would ever affect her again in such a way.

"Lea?"

She closed her eyes and said softly, "I'm leaving now, Karl."

He leaned forward placing both hands on the sink edge enclosing her within his arms, and buried his face into her hair. It felt as he had imagined—like the finest silk and her smell was as clean as a spring morning.

"We will meet again. Perhaps at the cabin?" he whispered, resting a cheek on her head. "We need to talk when you're ready. Dad will know where I am."

Lea knew when Karl left the room. She opened her eyes to the brightness of the morning sun. While mechanically soaping and rinsing the already clean sink with the small black sprayer that was attached beside the faucet, the steam rose into her face clouding her vision. Finally, she turned off the water, replaced the little black device into its holder, and turned to face the empty room. Karl's coffee cup still sat untouched on the table. She picked it up with both hands lifting it to her face to breath in the rich coffee scent. It was still warm. She only had to call out to him. He was still within hearing distance. Instead, she very, very gently placed the cup upon the table. It was time to go.

18

It was the last young gelding to exercise on her list. The morning sun was peaking over the tall palms that she had mentally named the three wise men. The position of the sun's rising had changed since she had begun her work there a month ago, getting her boss's three horses ready for their dèbut at the track.

After meeting him by chance one afternoon in an auction area in Tennessee, her boss had taken a liking to her conversation with a young man working at the auction yard. They were sitting in a barn on a bail of straw discussing the physical qualities of a bay stallion he had just seen sold for an outrageous price, a gamble for the buyer as the horse's offspring was not yet tested because of the stallion's young age. Still, the bloodline was an amazing mixture.

Jed Henderson, an unpretentious gentleman, had come up behind the two and stopped to listen to the young man question Lea on her past experiences handling a problem mount during a dressage competition some years back. As she was a listener around the old-timers wherever she went, Lea had learned some valuable ways to gain a young horse's confidence from the beginning of their training. The value of touch by brushing the animal and the pitch of one's voice proved most beneficial, but she was careful to point out the damage a handler could do if in too much of a hurry or temper to get the job done. Impatience was something to avoid at all costs.

Jed had lost no time in hiring Lea to minister to his racing stock. Not knowing of her past, only of her wish for privacy, he befriended her. Sending her with his racing team to California, she could now keep a low profile enjoying the somewhat undemanding work she needed so much.

Dressing the part of a stable hand/exercise girl, she soon blended with the group who accepted her as one the boss wanted to be "given her space but treated with respect." She soon became a quiet presence.

With no one constantly needing her, life's demands had become simplified. Lea enjoyed observing the movement around her and spending time with the magnificent animals she cared for. Her one day off a week was spent in church worship, hanging around her modest hotel room, and/or taking a bus to walk the beach or downtown streets. And while her slightly tinted glasses hid the extraordinary look of her eyes, they also gave her the needed freedom to study the everyday routine of the people she loved. Then combined with her clean but modest jeans, loose-fitting shirt, Levis' coat, work boots, and stocking hat—it was like being invisible.

Life had become routine—so easy—until now. The man she could almost avoid thinking about throughout the busy part of her day stood before her in the flesh. His intense blue eyes took in her appearance from her hat down to her tough leather work boots.

"You're not an easy one to find," he finally said.

Lea took him in, his very entirety from behind her eyeglasses. He was like a balm to the loneliness she had refused to acknowledge for so many months.

"Perhaps I did not wish to be found," she said.

In his way of smiling that was not a smile, she thought how it in no way could detract from his looks. In fact, she had missed the orneriness of it immensely. She had missed all of him. The perfection of his teeth, the military shaved cleanliness of every line of his face that she remembered as if etched on her brain by her very own touch, and his eyes that were a blue of God's own invention. She had just missed him.

"I've come a long way to speak to you. Have the courtesy to lose the shades."

"Speaking to a woman and with a woman are two different conversations altogether. If you're here to speak *to* me, you can get back into your army tank and back your way out of here."

"Woman you say? Have you bothered to look in a mirror lately?"

Lea leaned down to dig into her bucket for a curry comb. "Your parking meter is running out."

Karl closed his eyes in frustration. She was going to continue her avoidance of him. He had to hold on to something to be near her, to get her to understand that he was not a man to stop her from her ministry. He did understand what had gone on between her and her grandfather; and whether she knew it or not, their ending had been traumatic. She was afraid to love anyone too much again. The Lord was first in her life, and he respected her for it. In fact, her faithfulness made her the woman he wanted to be close to for the rest of his life. And he knew that he would be the one man to understand how to answer the loneliness he felt was so much a part of her life.

She was wary, her stubbornness the obstacle between them. But he too was stubborn, and defeat where she was concerned was not an option.

"So. You're going to ditch me again?"

Lea took a long, audible breath. "Karl. Karl. I *am* pleased to see you, my dear."

It was an effort not to laugh. *Was she the only one in life that he found truly funny?*

"My darling, Lea Ann. I have missed you." *And how he had missed that sassy grin these months!* "Would you allow me to hang around awhile? Take you to dinner occasionally. Meet some of your friends?"

Karl forced himself to breath as he watched her. She was thinking and miracle of miracles, she could not say no. But something was cooking up in that brain of hers, and it could not be good.

"Under one condition, Big Brother, *dear*. Let me introduce you to some ladies that might be of interest to you."

It was all Karl could do to keep his mouth closed in a dignified manner. Nothing she could have said should have surprised him! *So she thought to find him a wife? He had to say something or look quite stupid standing there in shock brought about by a twit of a girl! And him an accomplished psychiatrist who had heard of everything in the book!*

His mouth formed a slow, satisfied smile. "Alright," he said. "And if you have no luck getting rid of me after a few months' time, we will do some serious dating for at least one *year's* time. Yea. Just the two of us."

"*Six* months. I have six months to see if there is a lady out there meant for you? Okay?"

Karl reached out his hand to hers for a firm grip. "Deal, Little Sister."

Karl could only grin as he left the stables to find a motel. Lea would have her space and could do her best to find the perfect match for him. But one thing she had done unconsciously. She had broken one of her hard, fast rules—Lea made a promise to him and she *never* made promises.

In six month's time he would have her to himself to prove that she would have her freedom to live her ministry to their Lord Jesus Christ, and he would prove to her beyond a doubt, there was only one woman on God's earth that would ever be for him.